GW01164566

The Nine Deaths of Dr. Valentine

John Llewellyn Probert

Spectral Visions

spectralpress.wordpress.com

A SPECTRAL PRESS PUBLICATION

ISBN: 978-0-9573927-0-0

First edition, September 2012

Printed by Lightning Source, Milton Keynes

Editor/publisher Simon Marshall-Jones

Cover painting by JD Busch © 2012. Layout by Neil Williams.

Spectral Press, 5 Serjeants Green, Milton Keynes, Bucks, MK14 6HA

Website: *spectralpress.wordpress.com*

Dedicated to the memory of Vincent Price

I

The man's body was a writhing ball of fire.

Suspended a hundred feet above the river Avon by the chain that had been wound around his neck, the wriggling form bucked and twisted as it hung from the Clifton Suspension Bridge in the absolute blackness of the early March morning, creating a fiery inferno that could be seen for miles.

It wasn't long before somebody noticed it.

An hour later, and despite their best efforts, by the time local police and fire crews had hoisted the by-then lifeless smoking body back up onto the bridge, the press had already arrived on the scene.

Detective Inspector Jeffrey Longdon ran a hand through thinning hair and regarded the collection of television cameras and hastily-dressed TV reporters behind the police barrier with disdain. Behind him, the charred corpse was being loaded into an ambulance. At least they managed to do it before Sky News turned up, he thought with a hint of pride, before remembering that Sky didn't have a Bristol office and tended to be late for everything that happened in the area anyway. He ordered his men to keep the bridge closed until sunrise when forensics could give the place a thorough going over.

"Commuters from Leigh Woods aren't going to be happy, sir," said Sergeant Jenny Newham as a photographer with a particularly bad case of body odour tried to sneak past the barricade. She gave him the wagging finger treatment, and when that didn't work, employed the tried and tested upraised palm in his spotty face, which did the trick. "They all use the Clifton Suspension Bridge to get into Bristol."

"Fuck 'em," said Longdon, reaching for his cigarettes and realising his wife had hidden the packet again to help him in his attempts to give up. He took one of Newham's and borrowed her lighter as well. "Them and their gas-guzzling four by fours can get to work the long way down through the gorge. It's not going to hurt them." He took a deep drag and felt dizzy, forgetting that his sergeant's Gauloises contained about ten times the nicotine he was used to. He focused on his watch to try and stop his head from spinning.

"Sun won't be up for another hour, sir," Jenny said. "Do you want to wait for forensics to start work?"

Longdon shook his head and coughed before taking another drag. "Have they managed to wake Patterson up yet?"

"The pathologist?" She nodded. "Apparently he's on his way in."

"Good," said Longdon as they made their way back to the car. "I want to know everything about our victim. Not just what he died of. I want to know how old he was, what he was wearing, and if Patterson can manage it I even want to know what he had for tea."

*

"A hearty meal of fish, potatoes and some kind of green vegetable. Could be cabbage, possibly broccoli. Difficult to tell because of the gastric digestion of the soft parts. All that acid, you see." Dr Richard Patterson MBBS, FRCPath put the dead man's stomach back down. As he laid it on the porcelain dissection slab it made a squelching sound and some of the contents he had just been describing leaked out. Longdon rolled his eyes while Jenny stifled a gag. "But of course what you want to know is how he died."

"If it's not too much trouble, Richard," Longdon knew his pathology colleague was a bit of a performer and he liked to humour him as best he could, but it had been a long day so far and it was still only eleven AM.

"Well, the burns, obviously," said Patterson, indicating the blackened eviscerated corpse on the table. "They pretty much cover his entire body. And the costume he was wearing wouldn't have helped."

Longdon raised an eyebrow at that. "Costume?"

Patterson nodded vigorously. "Oh yes." He tapped the charred skin of the man's right forearm with a scalpel handle and was rewarded with an unpleasant cracking sound. "This isn't normal eschar." Jenny frowned and Longdon mouthed "scar tissue" at her as Patterson continued. "Your chap was dressed up in some sort of costume, head to toe, so that when he was set alight it melted into his skin as well as setting it on fire." Patterson grimaced. "Very messy. And very painful too, I should imagine."

"Head to toe you say?" Longdon wanted to get that straight. "You mean his head was covered?"

"Exactly," said Patterson. "Some sort of all-over body thing. You know, like a diving suit. I've sent a sample off to forensics but they may be a while because they'll have to sort out what is skin and what isn't, which is never very easy."

"Well as soon as you find out let me know," said Longdon, looking around the post-mortem room and wondering what kind of person enjoyed spending most of their working day in such a place. "Any idea if it could have been suicide?" he asked.

Patterson sniffed. "You'd have a better idea of that than me, Inspector. I suppose it's conceivable that he got himself dressed up, wound a chain around his own neck, soaked himself in petrol and jumped off the Clifton Suspension Bridge but it's all a bit elaborate for someone who wanted to do themselves in."

"Elaborate and bloody impractical," said Longdon, turning to leave. "No, this isn't a suicide, and it wasn't an accident either." He pointed at the blackened thing on the dissecting table. "I want a full report on my desk before lunchtime, not that I'm planning on eating anything after the morning I've had."

*

"Nothing from Missing Persons yet, sir," said Jenny once they were back in the inspector's office.

"Bloody typical," said Longdon, going straight over to check the coffee machine, which proved to be empty, as did the tin beside it he kept the coffee in. "Does someone keep coming in here and pinching my Hot Lava Java?" he said, snapping the lid shut.

"No idea, sir," said the sergeant with a smile. "But I do know you finished the last of the other packet on Friday before we left."

"So I bloody did," said Longdon, suddenly remembering. His eyes strayed to the half-empty jar of Nescafe by the kettle. He pondered the possibility for a whole ten seconds before shaking his head. "Anything from dental records yet?"

"Nothing there either, sir. According to Dr Patterson, the teeth that aren't melted are in excellent condition so there may not be a dentist with any record of him."

"So he took care of himself," said Longdon, "whoever he was." He sat down behind his desk and pondered whether or not to ring the Chief Inspector yet.

"You know what he'll say, sir," said Jenny.

"How did you know what I was thinking?" Longdon asked with the hint of smile.

"Because you're a born worrier," she said, returning it, "and talking to the Chief Inspector is the next thing on the list to worry about."

"Enough with the shrewd remarks, Sergeant," said Longdon, "let's just keep our fingers crossed that's all we have to worry about for now."

II

Dr Evan Pritchard made a point of getting home early that evening. It hadn't mattered that his last patient of the day had wanted to talk and talk, the persistent symptoms of her neuroses still failing to be controlled, either by behavioural therapy or by the drugs he had prescribed for her. Eventually he had found it necessary to curtail their already over-running session, and Mrs Violet Twelvetrees had not been impressed by his excuse for having to practically manhandle her out of his private rooms. Pritchard had thought it was a very good excuse, partly because he considered a wedding anniversary to a perfectly plausible reason why a man should want to get home, and secondly because, while he had constructed occasionally ludicrous falsities to get him away from more bothersome patients in the past, this one was actually true.

Which was why he was surprised when he got home to find the house in darkness.

"Miranda?"

There was no reply. Strange, he thought. Perhaps she was late home herself, but that made no sense. His wife hadn't worked for several years now, not since he had gained his consultant post, and it was hardly likely that she would have forgotten what the date was. He switched on the kitchen light and draped his jacket on the back of a chair. He was about to go upstairs when he saw the note that had been left on the pine kitchen table. The lilac paper (Miranda's favourite) had been folded once and his Christian name scribbled in purple ink (another of Miranda's little eccentricities) on one side. He opened it and read the message within aloud.

"Darling, don't worry, I haven't forgotten about tonight, especially not after last year." Last year was still a bit of a sore point, not least because he had not just forgotten their anniversary, but had been at a conference in Vienna when he should have been at home with her. "I just thought it would be more fun if we did something a little different, so I'm waiting for you. But not here. If it's gone 5.30 --" Evan looked up at the clock to see it was closer to six " -- then the chauffeur should be waiting outside to take you for a little ride, and at the end of it you'll find me, and an extra special surprise. So what are you waiting for? Lots of love, M."

Pritchard folded the note back up and put it in his pocket, frowning as he did so. It was definitely his wife's handwriting, but the style was unlike anything she had said to him for several years now. He allowed himself a wry grin. Perhaps she was trying to rekindle old passions, and if that was the case he had no objection at all. Outside, a car horn blew. He pulled on his jacket and grabbed his overcoat, just in case they ended up somewhere chilly. His grin broadened as he remembered the time in Paris when they'd ended up having an impromptu assignation by the Seine on a chilly March night just like this one.

He climbed into the back of the waiting limousine and was surprised to find another lilac note waiting for him. Enjoy the ride, my darling, said more of that elegant purple script, and when the car reaches its destination, just follow the trail to find me! Pritchard tucked that note away too and settled back as the car drifted through the Bristol streets. The driver was hidden behind smoked glass, not that Pritchard felt like conversation anyway, but he wouldn't have minded at least a clue as to where he was going and how long it might take to get there.

The journey turned out to be shorter than he was expecting. The car pulled onto the side of the road and the door was opened. Pritchard stepped out to find himself on an area of grassy parkland he recognised as part of the Bristol Downs. From where he stood by the roadside, stretching away and around the shadowy outline of a clump of conifers, led an avenue of candles that had been placed in glass containers to prevent the wind from blowing out their flames.

Well, she's gone to an awful lot of trouble, I must say, thought Pritchard, wondering if Miranda had perhaps caused some disaster and had needed to create an elaborate apology for it. Still, it certainly made a change from their usual arguments. As the car drove away he made his way along the avenue of flickering lights, stumbling a little on the uneven ground.

When he rounded the conifer trees his mouth dropped open in astonishment. He hadn't been sure what to expect, and while he had been trying to guess what this improvised path might be leading to, he was still taken aback by what he saw.

At first Pritchard thought he was looking at a giant inflatable horse floating in the air. Then, as he came closer, he realised it was a hot air balloon, and that it was not a horse but a unicorn. The wicker basket was made for one man, or two at a very tight squeeze. Stapled to the front was another lilac note.

All you have to do is get in, my darling, it said. I've prepared a very special surprise for us and all you have to do is let the very clever controls on this lovely balloon guide you there.

Pritchard looked up to see an arrangement of electronic devices fixed to the frame a couple of feet below the brightly burning gas jets. The balloon itself was filled with air and ready to ascend. He took another look at the note and raised an eyebrow. Miranda had been known to do crazy things like this, but that had been years ago, when they'd first met. All the same, he was intrigued, and not a little excited, by the prospect of what might happen next, and so he buttoned up his jacket and climbed in.

Without warning the guy ropes came free from their attachments, presumably triggered by some device that had been activated by his climbing into the basket. Pritchard marvelled: what remarkable things they could make nowadays! He gripped the edge of the basket as it began to ascend.

Soon he was floating over Bristol. He saw the Clifton Suspension Bridge and the Avon Gorge way beneath, the headlights of cars travelling along either side of it tiny pinpricks of light in the darkness. Then he was heading over Clifton itself and towards Bristol City Centre. He passed over the university and as he headed down Park Street he realised the balloon was beginning to descend.

It's a funny way to get to the Sheraton Hotel, he thought, that being the obvious destination to meet up for a romantic evening.

But the balloon didn't head towards the hotel. Instead the electronic devices hummed and burred, and Pritchard's journey took an abrupt right turn toward the imposing four storey, neo-Georgian building that stood close to Bristol Cathedral and took up one whole side of the area locally known as College Green. Pritchard knew it was the Bristol Council House, the building that acted as the city's seat of government. What he wasn't expecting was for the balloon to halt its progress just above the building at the end nearest the street.

Pritchard looked over. Just below him stood one of the two golden unicorn statues that were positioned on the roof at either end of the long curving building. He waited for a moment for the balloon to move on but it stayed put. He shook the basket in case something had got stuck. What on earth was he supposed to do here?

Two students crossing the green waved at him. He was tempted to shout for help but felt so acutely embarrassed that all he could do was wave back.

As soon as he raised his hand he felt something give way beneath him as the bottom of the basket opened and Pritchard fell through. The cheerful expressions on the passing students' faces turned to ones of horror as they watched the man who had just waved to them hang onto the side of the basket for dear life, his legs flailing beneath him. What they didn't see was the row of spikes that emerged from the basket's border that caused him to release his grip.

Pritchard fell no more than three feet. Unfortunately his fall was broken by the horn of the gilded unicorn beneath him, which penetrated his spine and passed through his body to emerge from his chest. Despite his injury his body continued to twitch as the unicorn onto which it had been skewered gradually turned a dark shade of scarlet, but by the time anyone managed to get to him he had long since stopped moving altogether.

III

"So you're saying that a unicorn-shaped balloon carried this man over the council building, dropped him onto a two-foot-long spike belonging to another unicorn and then flew away again?"

The student, whose name was Steven Cope, nodded in response to DI Longdon's question.

The inspector turned to Cope's girlfriend Helen. "And that's what you saw as well?" he asked. The girl nodded in agreement and pulled her coat tighter around her. The air on College Green had turned very chilly. "And at no point," he persisted, "did either of you see who pushed him out?"

"No-one pushed him out," said Helen.

"What do you mean?" asked Jenny, who was busy taking notes.

"There was no-one else up there with him," said Cope. "Or if there was they must have been a midget. That basket was tiny. Anyway, if there was they would have fallen out with him."

"Because the bottom of the basket actually opened so he fell through it?" Longdon sneered. "I've never heard anything so ridiculous in my life."

"Well, to be honest, I had never seen anything so ridiculous," said Cope. "The balloon wasn't even travelling in the direction the wind was blowing. None of it made sense."

Longdon leaned close to him. "And how much have you had to drink tonight?" he asked.

Cope was defensive. "Couple of pints at the pub," he said, and then looked at his watch. "And they should have worn off well before now."

It was close to three in the morning. A healthy crowd of onlookers and reporters, including Sky News this time, had arrived within minutes of the first mobile phone footage going up on YouTube. They had come to record, broadcast and just generally stare and point at the body of Dr Evan Pritchard as it was inexpertly removed from its gilded murder weapon. And so thus it was that Dr Pritchard's lifeless body was brought down to earth, albeit with the occasional wobble and scrape along the brickwork of the Council House. They were just loading him into the ambulance when a taxi pulled up and a glamorous but exceedingly distressed-looking middle-aged lady got out. She exchanged words with one of the officers at the police cordon, who brought her over to Longdon and Jenny just as they were dismissing the two students.

"Sorry to bother you sir," said the officer, "but this lady says she knew the deceased."

"Well that's a charming way to put it," the woman snapped, her eyes blazing. "I'm his wife."

Longdon looked at Jenny. "I wasn't aware we'd released any details to the public," he said.

"That hardly matters when something like this is all over the bloody television." Miranda Pritchard looked up at the bloodstained unicorn. "I recognised him as soon as the damn thing came on the news."

"Even upside down and bent backwards?" Jenny couldn't help but say.

Miranda glared at her. "Obviously you're not married or you wouldn't be surprised that one can sometimes come home to find one's husband in that kind of position, stark staring drunk and moaning about his job or his colleagues or some bloody patient he's been having trouble with. God knows I used to find him like that often enough."

Jenny resisted the urge to smirk as she said, "And the reason you didn't report him missing this evening was...?"

Miranda's face reddened. "I was with... a friend," she said.

"For a night of television watching, obviously," said Longdon.

"You're bloody rude, Inspector," spat Miranda.

"And you're holding up our investigation, madam," he replied with no less vehemence. "We'll need to see you at the station tomorrow for questioning of course, but while you're here perhaps you could explain these?" He held out a handful of crumpled lilac notes. "They were in his pocket. Apart from his wallet and keys they were all he had on him."

But Miranda was no longer listening. She was staring, speechless, at the slips of paper.

"Well?" said Longdon. "Did you write these?"

Mrs Pritchard nodded slowly. When she spoke next her voice was little more than a dry croak. "Yes," she said, before looking at the detective with tears in her eyes, "I wrote them. But over two years ago."

"You mean he kept them all this time?" said Jenny.

Miranda shook her head. "I wrote them," she said. "But not for him."

"For another... friend?" said Longdon.

"Yes, Inspector," said Miranda, the tears flowing now. "For another friend. Happy now?"

"We'll take a full statement from you tomorrow," said Jenny, who called over the officer who had brought Miranda across. "You'd best get some rest."

As the sobbing woman was led away Longdon lit his first cigarette of the day.

"You're not happy are you?" said Jenny.

Longdon exhaled loudly and looked up at the unicorn. The fire brigade had a ladder up to it now and someone was trying to clean all the blood off.

"This city has just seen two elaborately planned murders in two days," he said. "If you want me to go further I'd add 'unnecessarily complicated' and 'ridiculous' to the description but that's strictly off the record. And I'm sure you don't need to ask me if I think they're linked. No, Sergeant Newham, I am not happy, I am not happy at all." Longdon threw his cigarette down and trod on it. "The only thing I'm hoping at the moment is that it's over."

IV

If DI Longdon hated one thing more than being in charge of morning briefings, it was conducting them after he'd had no sleep the night before.

Sergeant Newham had done him the inestimable service of popping into the Starbucks on the corner beforehand to get him a couple of double espressos. He accepted the tiny paper cups with a grunt before doing his best to give her a warm smile. She was a good girl and was doing a hell of a good job putting up with him in what the press was already beginning to call 'The Death Plunge Murders'.

'Police Baffled!' said one tabloid, a phrase Longdon thought had gone out in the 1950s.

'Police No Further in Bristol Death Probe,' said the Telegraph, which was honest without being unkind.

'Is This What We Pay Our Taxes For!!!' the Daily Mail had screamed while guiding its readers to pages two through five for the in-depth story of the Bristol police force's catalogue of blunders and mistakes over the last five years. No doubt guaranteed fact-free, thought Longdon, and put together with the sole intention of getting the wrong sort of people's blood boiling. Not that any of that mattered. There was a murderer at large and he needed results. He knocked back both coffees, got to his feet and called for order.

The assembled officers stopped chatting and regarded Longdon with respect. He knew it was really because they were all relieved they weren't standing where he was, in charge of a murder case that already had national press coverage and absolutely no leads.

"Ladies and gentlemen," he said, "thank you for coming." There were a few appreciative chuckles at that. "As you know, for the moment the Chief Inspector has allowed me to remain responsible for this case. Whether that's because he thinks I'm the best man for the job or the most disposable member of staff to carry the can when this all goes tits up I have no idea, but that doesn't matter." He turned to the pinboard behind him that summarised the information they had so far. "What does matter is that we need to find whoever's responsible for these murders before he - or she - does it again."

A young man with thinning sandy hair in the front row raised his hand and identified himself as Detective Sergeant David Kinsey. “Are we sure the murders are connected, sir?” he asked.

Longdon shrugged. “To be honest, no. The mode of death in each case was different but outlandish enough in both to conceivably be the work of the same person. Our psychologist Dr Diana Weston --” Longdon pointed to a smartly dressed young woman with dark hair pulled into a tight bun and spectacles that were much too large for her small face “-- is working hard putting together a profile of the killer’s thought processes based on what we have found so far. I understand she isn’t quite ready to present her findings yet.” The girl shook her head and looked down at the bulging file on her lap. “But I’m sure she will at the earliest opportunity. Now, if there are no further questions,” Longdon turned back to the board. “The first victim was discovered two nights ago hanging from Clifton Suspension Bridge in a state of immolation.”

The door banged open. Longdon rolled his eyes at the interruption and was about to release a barrage of abuse at the interloper until he realised it was the pathologist.

“Ah, the good Dr Patterson,” he said. “I hope you’ve got some information of use to us.”

Richard Patterson waved the manila file he was holding at Longdon. “I’ve got the post-mortem findings on our late Dr Pritchard,” he said. “He died of massive blood loss caused by puncture of the aorta and inferior vena cava by a heavy metal object thrust through his back just to the left of his first lumbar vertebra.”

“Nothing surprising there, then,” said Longdon. “But I was rather hoping you might have unearthed a bit more about our first victim.”

Patterson looked confused. “Haven’t you seen my report?” he said.

Longdon shook his head. “I only know what you told me the other morning in the autopsy room,” he said.

“But I sent you an email! I was here until God knows what time last night typing it.”

“Which probably explains why I haven’t read it yet, seeing as I was unexpectedly called to our impaled friend at the Bristol Council House,” said Longdon, aware that this exchange was being watched keenly by his assembled team. A couple of them at the back even appeared to be taking notes.

"Well, you might want to read it when you have a minute," said Patterson, turning to go.

"Just a minute, doctor." Longdon could sense all eyes were on him. "In case you hadn't noticed, we are having a morning briefing here. Anything you might have to say could help us with the case. I'd very much appreciate it if you could summarise what you've found for us now."

"You might want to read what I've said yourself before releasing it to your men," said Patterson. "It's a bit odd."

Longdon knew he was going to start shouting in a minute. "I'm sure it can't be much more 'odd' than what we've already had to deal with, Doctor," he said. "So if you would be so kind?"

Patterson cleared his throat, looked at his shoes as if pondering something for a moment and then said,

"Well, if you insist. As you know, the man's body was completely covered in full-thickness burns, and you may remember I mentioned to you that he seemed to be wearing some sort of suit." Longdon nodded. "Well, I sent samples off to the laboratory and they confirmed that what they received was a mixture of skin, rubber, and something else which they eventually concluded was the charred remains of synthetic hair fibres. Black ones. These were all over his body except for his face, where the rubber was of a different consistency." Patterson took a deep breath and looked at the sea of faces watching him. "The design and the rubber used were of a make commonly associated with certain brands of fancy dress outfit, and therefore, from the consistency and distribution of the synthetic hairs, it would seem that when the victim died he was most likely wearing a gorilla suit."

Longdon eventually broke the silence that ensued. "A gorilla suit?"

Patterson nodded. "Combining their findings with mine, our victim was probably wearing the gorilla suit when he had petrol poured all over him. The chain was then put around his neck, after which he was set on fire and pushed off the Clifton Suspension Bridge."

If Patterson had been a performer in a play he could not have got a better reaction from his audience. Hardened veterans and newcomers alike shifted uncomfortably in their seats at his calm clinical description.

"And do we have any further clues as to his identity?" Longdon asked.

Patterson shrugged. "No fingerprints, no distinguishing marks, not even eye colour to go on," he said. "Even the inside of his mouth was so badly scorched that quite a few of his teeth had either been dislodged or had melted, so comparison with dental records is proving difficult as well." The pathologist glanced at the room full of thoroughly uncomfortable police officers before turning back to Longdon. "Can I go now, please?"

Longdon nodded and turned back to his team. "Now you all know as much as I do," he said. "So far this lunatic has murdered a respected psychiatrist and an unidentifiable other, in both cases using means so far removed from what one might grudgingly describe as normal murder that we can only assume that he's clever." He looked at Dr Weston, who nodded. "And resourceful." She nodded again. "And, as you have no doubt already guessed, my major concern is whether or not he has any more planned. Well, I want us to be ready for him. Get out there and don't rest until you've found something that can either lead us to him or give us an idea of what he might be planning next. I don't want to be reading tomorrow about another poor bastard who's been bumped off in the kind of way you should only see in a Road Runner cartoon."

V

"Martin, where are you going?"

Dr Martin Davies closed the front door and looked back down the corridor of his lovely home to where his wife Wendy was looking at him admonishingly. He cursed to himself. It didn't look as if he was going to get to see Tracy this morning after all.

"I just thought I'd pop into the hospital and--"

He wasn't allowed to finish his sentence.

"Martin," said his wife, advancing on him with the spatula she had been using to cook the kids' scrambled eggs. "What day is it?

"Saturday," he said, trying hard not to avert his eyes from hers.

"And what," she said in a voice that was so quiet so as not to disturb the children and yet at the same time was positively terrifying, "did you promise Jemima and Jocasta you were going to do today?"

Now Martin had to think. He was sure he had promised to take his two daughters somewhere, but hadn't that been last weekend? Or the next one? From the look on Wendy's face it was obviously this one. He looked at his wife. Her black hair was tousled and she was wearing her favourite weekend grey leggings that were wearing out. She had that black T-shirt on that made her breasts stand out in a way he never let her know for fear she might stop wearing it. Even when she was mad at him she was beautiful, perhaps even more so. Perhaps it was time to call it a day with Tracy, he thought. He tried to stop thinking about both women and remember what he was supposed to have promised the girls.

It was Jocasta, his seven-year-old, who saved him. From behind the closed kitchen door she called, "When's daddy taking us to the zoo?"

"I knew that," said Martin in a tone of voice that patently betrayed him as not having had a clue.

Wendy was inches from him now, and raised the spatula so it was almost touching his nose. "You know what I ought to do with this, don't you?" she said. Martin could only nod. "And the only thing that's stopping me is that I know you'd like it too much."

He didn't know what to do and so he kissed the tip of her nose. Wendy giggled.

"You're a bloody naughty man, Martin Davies, wanting to go to that place which owns you body and bloody soul for most of the week." Martin was about to make his excuses but she held up a hand. "I know, you just want to go and make sure your patients are all right and believe me, I think it's admirable that a paediatrician should show such concern for his children there. But how about showing a bit of dedication to your children here. You know, your actual children? The ones I gave birth to after you spent some not inconsiderable time--"

Martin shushed her and pointed over Wendy's shoulder. Jemima had opened the kitchen door. His nine-year-old was standing there with her arms folded.

"Daddy," she said. "Jocasta keeps wanting to know when we're going."

"Just as soon as you've washed your hands and got your coat on," said Martin, looking at his wife, "isn't that right, Mummy?"

"That's right," said Wendy, "and just as soon as Daddy gets his coat on and gets the car out of the garage." She looked back at him. "Isn't that right, Daddy?"

A quarter of an hour later, and with the two girls safely secured in the backseat of his Lexus, Martin Davies was headed for Bristol Zoo.

*

The car park was almost full by the time they got there, even though it was only a little after half past nine. Martin cursed his forgetfulness as he did his best to squeeze between a Land Rover and a minibus that asked if several feet could be left next to it to allow disabled passengers to alight. They never need all that and besides, we'll probably be around and finished before they get back, Martin figured, letting the girls out and ensuring the car was locked.

"Can we go and see the squiggly things, Daddy?" said Jocasta, pointing at a sign that had been erected near the entrance.

Quite why his younger daughter had developed such a fascination for invertebrates, and in particular the kinds of creatures that would make Wendy scream and which Martin himself would prefer not to get too close to was anyone's guess. He looked at the poster displayed prominently next to the entry turnstiles. 'Today's Special Attraction!' it said in bubbly day-glo lettering, followed by, in the kind of shaky shimmery scary font Martin thought had gone out of fashion in the nineteen-seventies, 'The Creepy Crawly Creature Feature!' Coiled around the words were rather intimidating-looking cartoon depictions of centipedes, spiders and scorpions, all of which appeared to be attacking the words that were advertising them. At the bottom of the poster, in the far more friendly day-glo letters again, were the words 'Presented by Everyone's Friend, Captain Clowney!'

"Please!" said Jocasta, in the way only a seven-year-old girl who knows how to get her own way with her father is capable of. "And it's with Captain Clowney! Please please please!"

Martin had heard great things about Captain Clowney from Jocasta following the last time Wendy had taken them along to one of his zoo shows, allowing Martin to spend another couple of exhausting but rewarding hours with Tracy. That time it had been about monkeys. Or was it penguins? Anyway, trust Wendy to get lucky with something vaguely acceptable and for him to end up with the chamber of horrors.

"Do you want to go and see all the creepy crawlies as well?" he asked Jemima, who nodded enthusiastically.

"I don't like some of the things on that poster," she said. "But I do like Captain Clowney. He knows a lot about animals."

"All right then," said Martin, handing over his credit card to pay the admission price and asking for tickets to Captain Clowney's Creepy Crawly Creature Feature as well. The girl behind the booth tore off several strips of paper which she handed to him before activating the button that allowed the three of them through the turnstile. Martin just had time to glance at the poster again and note that the performance was scheduled for lunchtime before they were through. He looked up to see Jocasta already heading for the gift shop and a whole world of plush animals that she most definitely did not need any more of.

"Come back here, Jocasta," he said and then, when he beheld her glum face, "there'll be plenty of time for that later. Besides, how do you know Captain Clowney might not have cuddly centipedes and scorpions for sale at his show?"

"You can't cuddle a scorpion, silly," said Jocasta, the gift shop already forgotten as Martin set off with Jemima holding his left-hand and Jocasta his right for a leisurely tour of the animal enclosures.

They took in their favourites (the lions and tigers for Jemima, the monkeys and vultures for Jocasta, who had liked the singing ones in Disney's The Jungle Book) and stopped for crisps and Coke. It was surprisingly sunny for the time of year and they sat outside the cafeteria, the girls slurping noisily from their drinks bottles. Martin wished they sold something a bit stronger than just lemonade as he realised the time was edging ever closer to Captain Clowney's Hell On Earth for People Who Frankly Didn't Like Creepy Crawlies One Little Bit. Martin had never really considered himself to be such a person, but he did jump when he saw any spider larger than a fifty pence piece. And anything that buzzed near him would be frantically swatted away for fear that it was a wasp, even when it wasn't the season for them.

He sat and watched a line of ants rescue fragments of a crushed fruit pastille from beneath their seat. That was the size of insect he was comfortable with, and he had a feeling - a horrible, gut-churning feeling - that the Captain Clowney show was going to be one of those things that featured audience interaction. Which always meant the dads. Which meant he might get dragged up in front of everybody where the frank and utter terror of having some hideous wriggling thing waved in front of his face or put on his shoulder would be so obvious to everyone that he would never be able to set foot in the hospital again in case any of his staff had been in the audience.

"Are you all right, Daddy?" said Jemima, putting down her empty crisp packet.

"I'm fine, my love," said Martin, realising that he was sweating. He took out his handkerchief and mopped his face. "It's just a bit warm out here, that's all."

"No it isn't!" said Jocasta. "It's cold. Can we go and see the creepies now?"

Martin looked at his watch. Twenty minutes to go. "I suppose we could go and find where it is and get some seats," he said, getting to his feet with some difficulty as his legs seemed to have turned to water. He wobbled a bit and Jemima took his hand.

"Oh, Daddy, stop being silly!" she said as the two girls guided him past signs pointing to where Captain Clowney would soon be waiting.

The Insect House was a self-contained building the size of the cafeteria they had just left and was, to Martin's relief, situated just five minutes' walk away. Martin peered up at the massive anthropomorphic beetle that smiled down at him from above the entrance and felt a twinge of dread deep within his soul. On either side of the sheet plastic swing doors were signs announcing the special show at twelve that would be admission by ticket only.

"Come on, Daddy!" said Jocasta, oblivious to Martin's obvious reluctance to go in. The two girls pulled him through the swing doors where a chubby girl in a green shirt took their tickets.

"If you go in and through the door to your right you'll find there's plenty of room inside," she said with a smile. "Sometimes it's good to be early."

Martin didn't want to be early. He didn't want to be there at all, he now realised. But there was no turning back. All he could do was hope and pray that he didn't get singled out for any audience participation. Maybe if they sat at the back and kept quiet--

"Can we sit at the front, Daddy?" said Jocasta the minute she saw him edging to the back of the auditorium. "Please! I won't be able to see anything from up there."

The room in which they found themselves looked like a small lecture theatre, with the back half being taken up with rows of banked seating that had been arranged on scaffolding. At the front was a brightly lit performance area whose yellow papier-maché contours had presumably been constructed to resemble the arid dunes of the desert.

It was only when Martin had made sure his daughters were settled and he had sat down that he noticed the throne.

It was placed dead centre at the very back of the stage, and was the only feature other than the desertscape. Quite why it was there, or what part it might play in the proceedings, Martin wasn't sure, and it was only when he squinted to focus on it that a shiver scuttled along his back bone.

It was in the shape of a giant golden scorpion.

The backrest formed the curling tail, the massive stinger poised as if to pierce the skull of whoever might dare to sit on the rich velvet upholstery. The arms ended in open claws, pointing upward, the red leather lining of each presumably indicating that the unfortunate victim was meant to rest their arms in the claws themselves. Eight gilt legs emerged evenly from the seat. From its place at the back of the stage the scorpion throne probably looked very regal and very imposing.

To Martin it looked terrifying. In fact, the only thing more terrifying than the throne itself was the fact that it was enclosed on all four sides by transparent perspex, forming a cubicle with a door at the front.

Martin looked around him. The place was beginning to fill up, mainly with families, but there were a few large, almost uncontrollable, parties of under-tens with just one or two adults to stop them from running hither and thither, spilling the drinks and snacks he was sure he had seen a sign forbidding the bringing in of, and trying to solve the insurmountable problem of who wanted to sit with whom.

"How much longer, Daddy?" said Jocasta.

Martin looked at his watch and another wave of fear flooded over him. "Just five minutes, my love," he said, squeezing her hand more for his comfort than for hers.

She pulled his head close and whispered, "Don't worry, Daddy. It'll all be over in a bit."

Martin smiled at his perceptive daughter and was just about to tell his two girls just how much he loved them both when the house lights went down and a frivolous voice boomed over the loudspeakers.

"Who's it time for?"

"Captain Clowney!" responded those in the audience who had obviously been to one of these before, Martin's children included.

"He can't hear you," said the voice. "Who's it time for?"

Again the response, so raucous and shrill this time that it bordered on the hysterical.

"Well, here he comes!" It was all the excuse the children in the auditorium needed to scream and shout, stamp their feet, drop their drinks and generally make a mess of themselves at the altar of the man who came bounding on to the stage from the left.

Martin had never liked clowns. Even as a child the one reason he hadn't wanted to go to the circus with his parents was because of the so-called funny men. If they were so silly and friendly and happy, he had reasoned, why did they need to paint their smiles on? Somehow he had gone from that to deciding it was because they'd forgotten how to really smile and had to remind themselves by looking in the mirror at the painted one before they came out onto the stage.

If ordinary circus clowns scared Martin, Captain Clowney was a new experience in terror. Possibly the most disconcerting thing of all was that he was dressed all in white, like some sort of demented antiseptic entertainer on a high risk diseases ward. His white jumpsuit and boots were almost hidden by the ankle length white cloak he wore, a flamboyant garment that had been decorated with glittery crescent moons, stars and tiny ringed planets. His face was white as well, with his lips and eyes encircled with the kind of rouge that made Martin think of a badly painted ventriloquist's dummy. But the worst was the hair - a huge fluffy shock of ginger that had been scattered with glitter and teased through the holes in the headgear the captain was wearing so that it looked as if his head was exploding through his cap.

"Good morning, boys and girls!" he said. His voice was vaguely effeminate or possibly deliberately campy, and betrayed a hint of an American accent.

The response to his greeting was deafening.

"And who am I?"

There was another grating outburst as the assembled youthful throng chanted his name.

"That's right," said Captain Clowney, before adding with a big wink, "and mums and dads in the audience can just call me George."

Martin groaned and then found himself laughing at the joke, if only because he needed something - anything - to help relieve the tension.

"And what are we going to see today?" Captain Clowney asked.

"Creepy crawlies!!" the children responded in the kind of singsong monotone that always creeped Martin out, suggesting as it did the presence of some kind of infantile hive mind.

"That's right," said the clown, holding up his hands and wiggling his fingers while making scary noises. "Creepy crawlies. Would you like to see one now?" The audience response was as predictable as it was loud. "Good. Well in that case what I want you to do is help me call my good friend Natasha onto the stage because she's helping me look after all the creatures we're going to be seeing today."

Natasha was the girl who had taken their tickets on the way in. She climbed onto the stage still dressed in her regulation uniform, but now she was carrying a plastic box the size and shape of a large Tupperware container. She placed it on the small green baize-topped folding table Captain Clowney brought centre stage. Martin could see things moving in it. Now he was really wishing they hadn't sat in the front row.

"Let's start with something really wriggly!" said the Captain, taking what looked like a pair of baby salad tongs from one of the pockets of his cloak and lifting the lid of the glass box.

Martin recoiled as a squirming centipede was taken out of the container. Its body was as thick as his thumb and as long as his outstretched hand. The room was thrown into such a state of hush that he swore he could hear the creature's mandibles clicking against the device that held it.

"You won't find this in your garden at home," said Captain Clowney as the thing continued to wriggle. "It's from Brazil." He paused and looked around the room to ensure he had everyone's attention before continuing. "And it's very, very poisonous!"

If nothing else, Martin was impressed with this man's ability to turn a room full of restless anticipant children into one in which a pin dropping in the back row could have been detected. But wasn't it a bit irresponsible playing with something like that with youngsters present? Martin turned round and could see from the worried looks of some of the parents that they must be thinking the same thing.

"Before any of you get worried, perhaps I should say that my friend Natasha has reassured me that this little fellow has had all the poison taken out of him before today's performance," said the Captain. The collective adult sigh of relief was almost palpable. "Of course if I were to drop him he might scuttle up someone's trouser leg!"

The clown pretend-fumbled the angry-looking creature to a few accompanying audience gasps before returning it to the case.

More examples followed, all seemingly selected for their ability to inspire terror rather than for any real attempt at education, although Captain Clowney was sure to mention the country of origin and of course the dangerousness of the succession of giant beetles, hissing cockroaches and oversized locusts which followed. Some respite from the grotesques was provided when a tank featuring moon moths was brought in and one little girl from the audience had one settle on her finger after it had been treated to a dab of pheromone by the Captain. Then came the part Martin had been dreading.

"For our next demonstration we need a volunteer." Captain Clowney waved away the forest of infantile hands which immediately went up. "No. This time I need an adult volunteer," he said, his eyes scanning the audience. "One of you mums or dads who are feeling particularly brave, who fancy showing their kids that there's nothing to fear from one of the most terrifying creatures that lives in the desert!"

Martin could feel Jocasta poking him in the thigh but he kept his hands by his sides. Let some other poor bugger get shown up, he thought. I'm not going anywhere near that stage.

"We need someone to be the Scorpion King!" said Captain Clowney, indicating the throne Martin had seen earlier. And there's no way at all that I'm going near that, he thought to himself as the captain added, "Or Scorpion Queen, of course. Now, who is prepared to come out here and show everyone what they're made of?"

Hands were being tentatively raised now, but the Captain didn't seem to be too taken with the choices on offer. He teased at plumes of his copper hair as he looked around the room. Martin tried hard to shrink in his chair as the clown's gaze swept along the front row...

... and came to rest on Martin.

"You, sir!" said the Captain, holding out a white-gloved hand.

Martin shook his head, but the Captain was insistent.

"Oh come now, sir! Surely you wouldn't want to pass up an opportunity to be the Scorpion King in front of your lovely daughters and all the other boys and girls and ladies and gentlemen here?"

"Go on, Daddy!" said Jemima, her nine-year-old voice already tinged with embarrassment at her father's reticence. Behind him, Martin could feel the relief from those already lowering their hands, safe in the knowledge that someone else had been picked to go up on stage.

"Come on, my dear fellow," said the clown, who now seemed less funny than ever, "we mustn't keep everybody waiting, must we?"

Martin got up, even though his feet weren't too keen on the idea. He followed the Captain to the perspex box. The clown made a show of reaching into his voluminous cloak, from which he produced a gold key. He held it up to the audience.

"The key to the kingdom!" he said, unlocking the door and opening it to allow Martin to gain access. "Now, if the king would be so kind as to take his place upon his throne." Martin turned to look at the audience, at Jocasta and Jemima, so proud of their daddy for whatever doubtless embarrassing stunt he was about to be subjected to, and realised he had no choice but to sit on that horrible-looking chair.

"Arms in the rests, please," said the Captain, indicating the leather-lined open claws. "We need to have our king looking regal."

Was it Martin's imagination or was there now more than a hint of menace in the clown's voice? He shifted uncomfortably on the chair before grudgingly placing his wrists between the golden scorpion's pincers. Martin knew he was shaking but he was trying his damnedest not to show it front of everybody.

When the pincers clicked shut he yelped.

"Goodness me, goodness me," said Captain Clowney to the audience. "It would seem our pretender to the throne is a little distressed at what I have done." He turned to Martin. "Let me just reassure him and all of you that it is merely for his personal safety, and for the safety of any of the harmless little creatures that may soon be finding their way into the Scorpion King's domain." Martin was terrified now but he didn't dare back out and face being a laughing stock in front of his children. Captain Clowney ignored him and went back to addressing the audience.

"Every ruler must undergo a test. Every king must earn his crown. So it was in the days of ancient Egypt when this rite was performed on young princes before they could ascend to rule after their fathers had died. The ancient Egyptians had a name for it." Captain Clowney paused for maximum dramatic effect. Martin was on the verge of demanding to be released but the clown was too quick for him. "They called it 'The Trial of the Scorpion'!"

There was an intake of breath from the audience. Some children were so close to the edge of their seats that one in the back row actually fell off.

"But just to reassure everyone, and not least our young prince here," said the Captain, "the scorpions I'm going to place in here are absolutely harmless and cannot even sting. This is just a bit of fun to show you the kind of thing they used to do in the olden days."

When he said those last couple of words Captain Clowney gave Dr Martin Davies such a look of sheer hatred that Martin actually drew in breath to scream. He was only stopped by the Captain saying "When you've had enough, just yell and I'll let you out."

Then the Captain locked the door.

"Another mere precaution, ladies and gentlemen," he said. "The zoo would be most displeased with me if they were to lose any of their prize specimens and I myself would be mortified if any were to go missing."

Martin struggled. He could hardly move. What's more he could no longer hear what the clown was saying. Perhaps the box he was in was soundproof. The white figure waved his arms around dramatically before pointing above him. Martin looked up to see an open pipe. The mad bastard wasn't really going to drop scorpions on Martin's head, was he? Not in front of everyone, not at a kid's matinee show.

He felt something land lightly on his forehead. It tickled, then it scratched.

Then it stung.

Outside the clown kept talking and gesturing as Martin felt the spot that had been pricked suddenly become numb. The numbness spread from his temple, over his ear, down the side of his face and into his throat with such rapidity that by the time his brain had told his mouth to scream he couldn't.

Another something fell past his face and landed on his knee.

Martin couldn't move his head now, but out of the corner of his eye he could see a black scuttling shape that was trying to gain purchase on his worn jeans, trying with the two heavy pincers it had in front of its body. It didn't take long for the creature to get frustrated, and then raised its tail, the bulging black stinger poised to strike.

Pain like Martin had never known flooded his knee and spread rapidly up to his groin. His left leg kicked out involuntarily as more scorpions landed on it. Outside it looked as if Captain Clowney was encouraging the children to cheer at the braveness of the volunteer. The pain was everywhere now, little pinpricks of hell that were numbing and then burning his shoulders, his back, his hands.

He could even feel them crawling on his face.

He strained to look down and saw that the floor was now a sea of writhing darkness. Some of the creatures were starting to climb up the insides of his trouser legs. What had gone wrong? Had they brought the wrong scorpions along? Had that girl Natasha made a mistake?

No.

That wasn't it at all, Martin thought as he stared through watering eyes at the figure that was still cavorting gaily before the crowd. He thought he had recognised that voice, heavily disguised though it was, but had dismissed the idea as being impossible. But now, as he had no option but to watch the man who had disguised himself as Captain Clowney present Martin's death to an audience of under-tens he suddenly realised who it was who had locked him in here to be submitted to a long, slow and painful death in front of his own children.

And he realised he was doomed.

Through his now swiftly darkening vision he watched the man he had never thought he would see again give a final flourish of his cape before leaving the stage. The clown had probably told the audience he would be back in a moment to release his captive, but Martin knew he would be making good his escape.

It took a minute before anyone else realised what was wrong, and that was only because the sites of the multiple stings Martin had endured were beginning to swell in such a way that his face had suddenly taken on the appearance of a puffy, reddened meringue. Natasha took the key they had all seen Captain Clowney use and fitted it into the lock of the perspex cubicle.

It didn't work.

Now the children were screaming and security guards were hammering on the specially reinforced plastic. As his consciousness began to fade all Martin could do was say that he was sorry, sorry to Wendy for cheating on her, sorry to his children for not spending any time with them, and sorry to the man who had imprisoned him in here for what Martin and the others had done all those years ago.

VI

"You say you'd known him for a couple of years?"

A tearful Natasha nodded as there was a crash from behind them. Longdon turned to see two of his officers struggling with the body of the recently deceased Martin Davies.

"Sorry, sir," said Sergeant Newham. "We're having a bit of trouble getting him out."

"Yes I can see that," said Longdon as he watched his men trying unsuccessfully to pull the doctor's dead, swollen body through the doorway to the cubicle. After the room had been cleared and the police called, the fifty-seven scorpions they had found in the cubicle with the late doctor had been anaesthetised and taken away by the zoo's veterinarian to ensure that they hadn't been harmed.

Removing Dr Davies himself, however, was proving to be a more difficult matter.

"It's because he's so puffed up," said the sergeant.

"Well, get someone to take the bloody perspex apart, then," said Longdon irritably, before turning his attention back to Natasha. "And you say you had no idea he was going to do this?"

The girl shook her head. "He said he was going to do some kind of routine with that throne, but nothing like this. I don't even know where he got the scorpions from."

Longdon frowned. "What do you mean?" he said. "Don't they belong to the zoo?"

Natasha blew her nose and wiped her eyes again. "No. We've got a couple of Asian forest scorpions because they're quite big and black and look scary, but their venom isn't all that dangerous." She glanced at the box behind them and at the police force's increasingly clumsy efforts to extricate the oedematous body of Dr Davies. "We don't have anything that could do something like that."

"So we have someone who didn't just plan this murder but brought along his own scorpions as well," said Longdon.

"And probably painted them," said Natasha.

"I beg your pardon?"

"Most poisonous scorpions live in the desert," Natasha explained, "so they tend to be yellow or orange to blend in. I'm not an expert but if he wanted to kill someone he'd have used something like that."

"Jesus Christ," said Longdon. Behind him the efforts of the Bristol police force finally met with success, and at last the body of Dr Davies was laid upon a trolley.

"He's going to droop over the sides a bit what with all that swelling," said one of the paramedics who were there to wheel him out. "Maybe we'd better put a couple of blankets over him."

"Yes, I think that would be a good idea," said Longdon, close to the point of exasperation. He looked around him. "Where's that bloody personnel officer?"

"Here, inspector," said a short bearded man whose badge proclaimed him to be Jim Burrows from the zoo's Human Resources department.

"Right, Mr Burrows," said Longdon, pointing to the wobbling trolley behind him, "perhaps you can tell me how the man who did that managed to pass all your no doubt rigorous security and child protection checks?"

Burrows shrugged. "Captain Clowney has an impeccable record, Inspector. He's been putting on shows here for a few years now, once or twice a month. He's become quite a favourite with the children."

Longdon failed to be convinced. "Presumably you have all his details on file?" he asked. "Real name, date of birth, contact address and so on?"

Burrows looked incensed. "Of course, Inspector. We're very careful indeed about who we employ here. All I can say is that there was nothing in his police check that suggested he was anything other than the most trustworthy of individuals."

"Well, just make sure you have all his records forwarded to my office," Longdon said before shouting across the room to his colleague. "Sergeant!" Jenny Newham looked up from supervising the removal and tagging of the perspex chamber as evidence. "When you've finished here, go and find out if those scorpions they took out of here were painted will you?"

Jenny looked confused. "Sir?"

Longdon ignored her as he swallowed hard and went to interview Davies' family.

*

By the time they got back to the station Longdon and Newham had had more than their fill of distraught relatives, irate zoo officials and unscrupulous members of the press keen to discover what gory horrors the Bristol Killer ("They're not just bastards, they're unimaginative ones too," Longdon had quipped as he moved the latest pile of dailies off his desk) had managed to come up with this time.

"Richard Patterson's in your office," the desk sergeant said to Longdon as he entered. "Says he's got some information for you."

"Let's hope it's a bit more useful than 'He was stung to death by scorpions'," said Longdon.

"Painted scorpions, sir," said Sergeant Newham with a winsome smile.

"Of course, Sergeant." Longdon could still see the horrified expression on the zoo officials' faces. Every scorpion that had been recovered from and around the body of Dr Martin Davies had died within an hour of being taken away. Something about the toxicity of the paint they had been dipped in to give them such a black colour.

"Probably made them mad as well," Natasha had said. "No wonder they stung him so much." Apparently the RSPCA were going to be involved and the zoo officials were not impressed when Longdon told them that was the least of his concerns. The two reporters who overheard his words, however, loved it, and scuttled off immediately to start constructing the next day's headline which would no doubt be along the lines of 'Blundering Detective Animal Hater As Well'. In the end they concentrated on the distress of Dr Davies' family in the light of his having been stung over three hundred times by a room full of lethal scorpions.

"What do you want now, Richard?"

The pathologist was sitting beside Longdon's desk. The coffee pot in the corner was bubbling away.

"I hope you don't mind but I took the liberty of putting some on" said the doctor. "I have a couple of things I need to talk to you about."

Longdon pushed back his desk chair and flopped into it. Jenny stayed standing in the corner.

"I cannot possibly let a lady stand," said Patterson, getting to his feet and letting the Sergeant have the chair. The pathologist perched on the desk, which creaked ominously.

"Well?" said Longdon after a suitable pause.

Patterson waved a thin manila document at him. "We have an ID on our first victim," he said. "An Andrew Wells, not of this parish, which is why it took us a little while to track him down. He works in Buckinghamshire where his wife filed a missing persons report on him last week."

"I don't suppose he was Dr Andrew Wells, was he?" said Longdon, already expecting the answer.

"No," said Patterson who, scarcely missing a beat, then added, "he was Mr Andrew Wells, a Consultant in charge of a local hospital Accident and Emergency department. Apparently he'd worked there for seven years."

"Three deaths, three doctors," said Longdon, leaning back in his chair and staring at the ceiling.

"I wonder what the hell they did to upset someone so badly?" said Jenny.

"More importantly," said Longdon, realising that if he leaned any further back his chair might fall over, "we need to find out if anyone else might have upset our killer as well. Get every single scrap of information you can about these three doctors and find out what it is that links them."

"Yes sir," said Jenny.

Longdon shooed her out of the room. "Now, Sergeant!"

Jenny Newham closed the door with a bang as she left.

"You shouldn't shout at her," said Patterson. "She's a good girl, and she obviously thinks the world of you."

"Then she isn't a very good judge of that sort of thing, is she?" said Longdon, trying to conceal the grin Patterson's comment had provoked. He looked at the bubbling coffee machine. "Was that all you had for me?"

"Not exactly." Patterson got up off the desk and poured them a mug each. "The other thing isn't exactly factual. In fact, I'm not really sure what to call it."

Longdon tried to take a sip but the coffee was too hot. "Richard, what are you going on about?"

There was a pause as Patterson seemed to be trying to decide whether he should speak up or not. Eventually he said, "It's not just the fact that they're all doctors that links these killings."

"What do you mean?"

Patterson sat down and waited for Longdon to follow suit before continuing.

"Do you watch horror films, Inspector?"

It might not have been the last thing Longdon had been expecting Patterson to say but it was close. "No," he replied, "never really been my thing, and certainly not the kinds of films that the press have been likening all this business to. When I was a kid I watched some Hammer films but this Saw thing they keep comparing the murders to doesn't sound like the kind of fare anyone sane should really be watching. And what is it about calling all this horror stuff after things you'd find in a toolbox? Anyway - why?" Longdon narrowed his eyes. "Are you a fan?"

"Oh good Lord, no!" Patterson rolled his eyes. "It's my daughter, actually. She loves the things. Can't watch enough of them. No idea what the appeal is myself but there we are. Anyway, it was after you rang me to do the autopsy on this latest killing that she pointed it out."

"Pointed what out?"

Patterson opened his briefcase and took out an A4 printout of a garish movie poster. Longdon looked at the face of the man depicted on it and didn't think he had ever seen so many different shades of red.

"I don't have the facilities at home but fortunately Vice has just invested in a new colour laser printer so I ran this off down there," said the pathologist, turning it round so Longdon could get a better look at it.

"Edgar Allan Poe's immortal masterpiece of the macabre 'The Masque of the Red Death'," Longdon read aloud before looking up at Patterson. "And this is important because...?"

Patterson made himself comfortable. "Because in Roger Corman's 1964 film The Masque of the Red Death the character of Prince Prospero, played by Vincent Price --" Patterson tapped the face on the poster "-- organises a party where the character of Alfredo, played by Patrick Magee, gets suspended in the air while wearing a gorilla suit. Which is then set on fire."

Longdon waited for Patterson to continue and then realised the pathologist was waiting for him to make the connection. "Like Dr Wells," he said.

"Mr Wells," Patterson corrected. "Surgical consultant, you see. They can get very upset if you don't get their title right. But yes - exactly like Andrew Wells."

Longdon took a swig of his coffee which at last was thankfully comfortable to drink. Where was Patterson going with this? "And this piece of random information helps us how, exactly?" he said.

Patterson took another sheet of paper from his briefcase.

"Love means never having to say you're ugly." Longdon read that tag-line out loud again before looking at the picture of a rotting skull-faced cadaver about to kiss a beautiful woman.

"In The Abominable Dr Phibes the character of Dr Phibes, played by Vincent Price --" again Patterson tapped the poster in case Longdon wasn't getting the idea "-- engineers the deaths of a number of doctors, and of particular interest here is the death afforded the character of Dr Whitcombe, played by Maurice Kaufman."

Longdon looked up at Patterson. "I don't suppose he's dropped out of a balloon, is he?"

The pathologist shook his head. "He's impaled on a brass unicorn head, Inspector."

"Like our Dr Pritchard?"

Patterson nodded. "Like our Dr Pritchard."

Another poster came out of the briefcase, this time of a woman's bleeding eye with a spider crawling across it.

"I'm not even going to read what that says," said Longdon, unable to bring himself to quote the poster's tagline of Flesh Crawls! Blood Curdles! Phibes Lives!

"In the sequel to The Abominable Dr Phibes," Patterson continued, ignoring his colleague, "rather unimaginatively titled Dr Phibes Rises Again, the character of Dr Phibes, yet again played by Vincent Price, causes the character of an archaeologist played by Keith Buckley to be stung to death by the same creatures that killed our Dr Davies while trapped in a throne that is itself fashioned in the shape of a giant golden scorpion."

"Oh bloody hell," said Longdon, putting his head in his hands.

"Bloody hell indeed, Inspector," replied the pathologist.

"And I suppose there are other films in which this actor kills people?"

Patterson nodded. "Apparently so, quite a lot of them in fact, which really puts the pressure on your Sergeant Newham to find out what the connection is between the victims so far or the press might find they're going to have stories for the rest of this month."

"More likely this year," Longdon groaned, stretching his arms. "So what am I supposed to do now? Call in a film critic?"

Patterson tapped the Abominable Dr Phibes poster again. “It might not hurt to at least get a book on these films so we can get some idea of what the killer might have in store next.”

“All right,” said Longdon. “I don’t suppose your daughter fancies coming in to help?”

Patterson shook his head and smiled. “She’s away at university, following in the footsteps of her father. I wouldn’t want her to be involved in this anyway and I certainly wouldn’t want it to interrupt her education. I’m sure you’ll be able to find someone locally who knows about these sorts of films. Although I’d suggest you make your inquiries discreet. There are a lot of very odd people around who like these kinds of things.”

VII

"Dr Parsons? I think Mrs Fudgsin's bowels have had a good result from that enema."

Lorraine Parsons dropped her cigarette and trod the burning ember into the tarmac, extinguishing it with a hiss. She turned to see the rotund face of practice nurse Garry Bellamy peering anxiously around the fire exit door. She knew that no-one, not even staff, was supposed to go through it 'except in cases of emergency', at least according to the practice's annual interminable lecture from that prig of a fire safety officer. Still, Garry wasn't going to tell anyone, not after what she had caught him doing with some of the items on the proctoscopy tray last month.

"All right, Garry," she said, following him back inside. "If you're happy with what she's managed to do, send her on her way with one more sachet. But tell her she's absolutely not to have more than half of it at a time, otherwise it'll be her husband they'll be carting off to casualty with shock, instead of his wife with a simple case of constipation."

"All right, Doctor." Garry sniffed and pointed to the door to Lorraine's consulting room. "Your husband's on the phone. He said he'd wait."

And you'd better not have told him why he's had to wait, thought Lorraine as Garry shuffled away, or else a few other people might find out what you get up to when you think there's nobody else here.

"Hello, Peter," she said once she had the surgery door closed.

The voice on the other end of the line didn't sound happy.

"Look," she said. "I can't do it. You know I've got this bloody thing to attend this afternoon. You'll just have to take Davinia to the Pony Prom yourself. No, I don't know what the hell a Pony Prom is either. Your daughter has probably got entirely the wrong end of the stick. After all," she said with a sigh, "she does take after you in so many ways. Yes, I love you too." She put down the phone, sending away the husband she didn't really love at all and the daughter she was coming to despise for her slow-witted ways, and looked at her watch. It was nearly one o'clock, which meant that with any luck her surgery hours were over for the day. A quick phone call to Martha her receptionist confirmed it, and after she had filed away her patients' notes from her morning consultations she turned her attention to the letter she had been sent through the post three weeks ago.

"Lavenham Productions would like to take great pleasure in cordially inviting you to participate in their reality television programme 'This Civil Life'. We are dedicated to reproducing, for one afternoon only, a famous period in history in a village of local importance. In order to increase the verisimilitude we are looking for professional people who would be willing to play the roles they do in everyday life now, but in an historic context. Consequently, lawyers, farmers, shop owners and others in your area have all been contacted in the hope that they will be willing to participate in this exciting project. Your cooperation and involvement in 'This Civil Life' would be greatly appreciated and, as we have already pre-sold the programme to a commercial broadcasting channel, we will be able to show our gratitude with a financial reimbursement for your time, which you may either donate to the charity of your choice or do with what you wish.'

Below that was her name and the details of the not inconsiderable sum of money to be paid into her bank account should she be willing to take part. Lorraine looked at the figure again and went over the numbers in her head for the umpteenth time. The money Lavenham Productions was willing to pay should be just enough to cover the gambling debts she had accrued on the Thursday afternoons when Gareth had thought she was doing her special learning difficulties charity clinic in Bristol. In fact, she had been at the racetrack trying to win back the money that should have gone on their summer holiday last year. Thank God Peter had no idea how she'd lost all that money. But never mind, she thought with a smile as she tucked the letter into her bag, if one afternoon of reality TV could pay for it all then why not? And it wasn't as if Peter watched any of that kind of stuff, so it was hardly likely she'd be found out.

The sun was breaking through the clouds as she got into her car and set off into the wilds of the Somerset countryside. March was starting off nicely, she thought, as she put on her sunglasses and turned up the stereo, and it was about to get even better.

She followed the map that had come with the letter, grateful that she had remembered to bring it as she was taken down ever more minor roads after leaving the M5. Eventually, as her car was scraping its way along the hedgerows of a single track, macadam-paved lane, and

Lorraine was dreading to think what the loose chippings were doing to the emerald green paintwork, and assuming she must have taken a wrong turn, the road suddenly turned a corner and widened.

And she found herself three hundred years in the past.

The town square into which she drove was large, and the ground had been matted with straw, presumably to cover up any road markings as well as to add to the authentic feel they were obviously trying to reproduce. There were people everywhere, many of them in period dress. A man in a very un-seventeenth-century long-sleeved shirt bearing the stovepipe-hatted logo of the production company came running over waving a clipboard. Once she had wound the window down she could hear what he was saying.

"I'm afraid this route is closed today," he shouted over the noise of whatever it was a team of carpenters were constructing in the middle of the square, "we're filming, you see."

"I know," said Lorraine, showing him the letter. "I think I'm supposed to be a part of it."

The young man's apologetic expression broadened to a smile. "Dr Parsons! Thank you so much for coming! We weren't sure if you were going to be able to make it. Andy Deacon - pleased to meet you."

"Well, I did ring to confirm," she said, shaking his outstretched hand.

Andy nodded. "Even so, we know that doctors can get unexpectedly called away. It's wonderful you've been able to make the time for our little production."

Lorraine eyed her presumed co-stars as they milled about. "It doesn't look that little to me," she said.

"By comparison with some of the things I've worked on," he said with a smile. "But you're right. They've really done a marvellous job with very limited resources here."

"Don't you mean you have?" she narrowed her eyes.

"Oh I've just been hired for the day as a production assistant," he said, looking behind him, "which is a shame really as this all looks such fun I wish I was on it for longer. Anyway, I'll show you where you can park your car and then we'll get you into costume and makeup."

The village (Lorraine still hadn't seen a name and the film company's map had simply marked it as 'Location') was so tiny that once she had, with Andy's help, negotiated her car slowly across the square and out the other side, she found herself past the tiny crop of buildings and turning left into a field where there were numerous other vehicles and a number of tents.

"All set up this morning," said Andy with a grin. "I'm always amazed at how quickly all these things come together. You wouldn't believe that at six o'clock none of this was here, would you?"

"So have you all been working on this somewhere else, then?" said Lorraine as they got out of her car.

Andy shrugged. "Not exactly. Independent production company, you see. We just get the phone call and turn up, a bit like you. I've worked with a few people on here before, but most of them I don't recognise. Apparently they want everything done by teatime which is why there's such a rush on. The money's phenomenal, though, so I'm not complaining."

Lorraine slammed the car door and locked it. "Which reminds me," she said, "when exactly do I--"

"Get paid?" Andy smiled. "It'll all be done by a bank transfer in a couple of days. Unless of course you'd prefer some other method?"

Lorraine shook her head. Thank goodness she had opened that private bank account that Peter knew nothing about. The fact that it was several thousand pounds in the red now just made it all the more appropriate for the money to go straight in there.

She was still thinking about what a shot in the arm this was going to be to her finances as Andy led her across the field towards one of the smaller tents.

"We'll get you into costume first and then sort out your makeup," he said.

"What period in history are we actually doing?" she asked.

Andy stopped. With the expression on his face she might have just told him she thought she was supposed to be on a cookery show. "You mean they haven't told you?"

Lorraine shook her head. "I just know the title 'This Civil Life' but they didn't tell me anything else."

"Oh my goodness, I'm sorry." They were nearly at the tent now as Andy turned round to point back to the village. "For one afternoon we are turning that collection of mouldy old buildings into a seventeenth-century village. The English civil war, you see?"

Lorraine nodded as realisation dawned. That explained the plethora of peasant costumes she had seen on the way in. "But what about the people who actually live in the place?" she said. "Have you sent them all away for the afternoon?"

Andy grinned. "All part of the magic of television," he said. "When the team arrived this morning there were a couple of tumbledown old farm buildings that hadn't been used in donkey's years. You'd be amazed what can be achieved with a few backdrops and some standing set scenery borrowed from the Pinewood backlot."

Lorraine squinted at the village in the afternoon sunlight. It was obvious now, of course. She had actually just driven through a set, and it had only been her expectations and assumptions that had led her to believe anything else. She smiled. "That's very impressive, you know," she said.

Andy did a little bow. "Nothing to do with me," he said. "Well, not much, but thank you anyway. Now come and meet Melissa."

Melissa was tall, had a shock of pink frizzy hair and a suspiciously deep voice. She got Lorraine to stand next to a full length mirror, stroked her chin, hummed and hawed and then took three scruffy looking dresses off a rack of the things that all looked the same as far as the doctor was concerned. She held each one up next to Lorraine while conducting a running conversation with herself.

"Too Kate Winslet," she said of the first, shaking her head and throwing it on a chair "and my God, you don't want to be likened to her do you? I mean, fifteen years ago, okay, but now that look is so out of date. Mind you, so is Meg Ryan." Now she was holding up the second dress. "I don't know why they've given me these to work with," she said with an exaggerated sigh. "I mean this isn't supposed to be Sleepless in Somerset, it's supposed to be real life. Let's try the third." Lorraine didn't like any of them but at least the third had a bit more to it. Melissa pursed her lips, "Hmmm. This one makes you look a little bit Rachel Weisz, especially if they use a soft focus camera on you, which of course they won't. Oh well." She handed Lorraine the dress. "Try it on and we'll see how it looks."

The only place to get changed was behind the rack of dresses, and Lorraine managed it in record time. Melissa seemed happy enough and passed her on to the next tent where a grumpy makeup artist called George made her hair look awful and added a couple of skin blemishes.

"They all had them in those days," he said when she protested about him trying to add a wart with hair coming out of it. Once he realised she'd be tugging it off as soon as she was away from there he gave up and sent her outside where Andy introduced her to Malcolm, who was a solicitor from Cheltenham and had been dressed up to look like something out of an Arthur Miller play.

"Are you excited?" he asked as they made their way back over to the mostly fabricated buildings. "I was delighted when I got the letter." It turned out he belonged to one of those historical re-enactment societies, which was apparently how quite a few of the people there had been recruited.

"Happy?" Andy asked once the two of them were back in the town square. Malcolm gave a delighted nod but Lorraine wasn't quite so sure.

"What am I supposed to do exactly?" she asked.

"Just play along," said Andy. "There's sort of a script to get things going and some of the people here are genuine actors, so all you have to do is react to what's going on."

Lorraine looked up at the wooden pole that had been erected in the middle of the square. "What's that for?" she asked.

"You'll see," said the production assistant. "I've been sworn to secrecy or else I don't get paid. The producer wants real reactions so he doesn't want anyone knowing too much."

In that case, the only reactions he's going to get from me are confusion and looking increasingly pissed off, Lorraine thought. Then she remembered the money and made herself calm down. But something else was bothering her. As she looked around she realised what it was.

"Where are the cameras?" she asked Andy just as he was leaving.

He gave her a big smile and pointed to the windows of various houses. "All concealed in there," he said, "so you don't have any distractions at all."

"I've got some lines." Malcolm was so excited he couldn't help but blurt out the words.

"Yes Malcolm, you have," said Andy, "but no telling Lorraine what they are, remember? Otherwise your historical society doesn't get that donation it's been promised." Malcolm looked suitably told off as Lorraine marvelled at how the production company had obviously managed to get what they wanted by offering financial reimbursement in all manner of ways. Andy looked around. "Right," he said. "I think we're about ready to go. I had a word with everyone else while you were getting ready. Our main star is offstage at the moment but once

I'm out of here the cameras will start rolling so we'll be needing you to just be yourselves."

"Be ourselves how?" Malcolm asked.

"Just talk about the weather or how you got here," was the reply. "You know, just general chit-chat. You'll know once the show has begun."

I'm more interested in knowing when it's over, thought Lorraine, although she guessed that would be obvious enough when the time came. She tried to make small talk with Malcolm as Andy dashed off behind the scenes, but the man already bored her, it was getting cold, her dress itched and she was keen to get the whole thing over with.

She didn't have to wait long.

"Bring forth that sorceress condemned to burn!"

The voice, whose deep booming tones carried over the mumbling crowd, came from beneath the arch in the far left-hand corner of the square. Everyone turned to see who had spoken, and Lorraine had to stand on tiptoe to be able to see the man to whom the voice belonged.

He was of medium height, but the black stovepipe hat he wore made him look taller. His garb was period perfect and the black cloak he wore swirled about him as he walked. As he reached the centre of the square through the parted crowd the voice boomed again.

"I say for a second time: where is the witch who by her foul deeds has committed herself to be cleansed by the purifying flames?"

There was a pause before Malcolm, still standing next to her, jumped in realisation.

"Oh my goodness, that's me," he whispered to her, before calling out to the sinister man in black, "I have her here, good my Lord."

"Then bring her to me that I might set eyes upon this evil harpy." His blue eyes glittered with a gleeful malevolence. Whoever he is, he's bloody good, thought Lorraine, wondering who it was who was destined to be subjected to his melodramatic overtures. As she did so she became aware that the crowd had separated itself from her as Malcolm had linked his arm in hers.

"Don't worry," he whispered. "Just play along. All part of the show."

"Me? What, no, get off!" Lorraine spluttered, but it was no use. Besides, if she spoiled it all there was a chance no-one would get paid and then she'd be in all sorts of trouble.

"Before me, my good man! Now, if you please!"

As meekly as she knew how, which admittedly wasn't very meekly at all, Lorraine allowed herself to be brought before the witchfinder, who made a point of keeping his distance from the accused. When she was pushed to her knees she offered some resistance but then she remembered she was wearing the costume department's rags so it didn't matter if they got messed up.

"Well, young lady," the black-clad man said. "Have you anything to say for yourself?"

There was a nudge behind her from Malcolm. What on earth was she supposed to say? And then she remembered. Be yourself, she had been told.

"I am a doctor, your worship," she said, hoping that was how one addressed a seventeenth-century witchfinder.

"A doctor!" That seemed to amuse him. "A doctor, she says!" Now he was addressing the crowd. "A woman healing the sick? In this day and age? I ask you, men and women of this village - have you ever heard of anything more absurd in your entire lives?"

There were lots of cries of "No!" and a few more worrying shouts of "Burn her!" as the crowd started to get into the spirit of the thing.

"I have healed the sick, sir," said Lorraine, also getting into the swing of it, "on many occasions, and with some success I might add."

"Coincidence, luck, or worse..." The witchfinder raised his voice for maximum effect at this point. "The work of the Devil! And of the Devil's own! And I see this particular servant of Satan does not even try to defend herself but willingly admits to her evil practices! For her there can only be one absolution!"

There were more cries from the increasingly enthusiastic crowd now, and for the first time Lorraine felt a pang of worry. She looked round and breathed a sigh of relief that she couldn't see a stake anywhere that she could be tied to.

When the crowd had died down the witchfinder spoke again.

"I therefore have no alternative but to pass sentence. The path of the righteous can be difficult, and we who do God's work perform it sometimes with the heaviest of hearts. Yet I say that to save this woman's soul she must undergo absolution by burning."

Lorraine could feel hands grabbing her now and she realised she couldn't move. She struggled and cried out as the witchfinder called for something called 'the frame'.

"Don't worry," Malcolm whispered to her as she was dragged forward. "They wanted to have a fire here but health and safety wouldn't let them. I heard them talking about it this morning."

Well, that's a relief, thought Lorraine as she allowed herself to be dragged to the centre of the square until she was close to the pole she had noticed earlier. It had to be at least twenty feet high. Were they proposing to tie her to that? And if so, why had they made it so high?

There was movement from the other side of the square. The crowd parted again as four men approached, carrying what looked to Lorraine like a ladder, about the same length as the pole. When they laid it on the ground she could see there were loops at one end for her hands and feet. Still held in a vice-like grip, she was turned to face the crowd.

"Mistress Lorraine Parsons," said the witchfinder from behind her, "you have been found guilty of the most heinous crime of witchcraft, of encouraging others to place trust in you and in claiming to have abilities which you did not possess."

Lorraine frowned. That sounded a bit odd. Shouldn't he have said 'do not possess?'

"For that I order that you be lashed to the frame, raised up and then lowered into the purifying flames so that all might see your just retribution at the hands of the Lord."

As he spoke Lorraine felt herself being lifted up and set down on the wooden frame. She struggled as they slid the loops of hemp over her wrists and ankles, not just because the frame was bloody uncomfortable but because she was starting to get scared.

But not as scared as she was when the witchfinder came round to face her.

He had kept his distance before but now there he was, right in front of her, an evil smile on his lips and malevolence in his eyes. However, neither of those was what struck a greater fear into her heart than she had ever known.

She recognised him.

It had been many years and he looked older, but she recognised him.

A man she had thought was dead.

"I will pray for you," he said, not looking as if he meant a word of it, and as they began to raise her up Lorraine realised that she wasn't going to be leaving this place alive.

That was when she started screaming.

"See how the guilty party now pleads for her life!" the witchfinder crowed as Lorraine was hoisted up. The crowd was now so worked up that it was impossible for her to make herself heard. "Secure the ropes!" he commanded, and within a few short moments Lorraine was twenty feet above them, lashed to the wood, cold, afraid, and already reduced to gibbering in terror. It was therefore unsurprising that the crowd ignored her as the witchfinder once again commanded their attention.

"This... woman has been found guilty of one of the vilest of crimes," he said, "and it is only meet and right that she be justly punished for it." Suddenly his voice changed and became far less theatrical. Suddenly it was just the man who was playing the role who was speaking to them and the effect was more than a little disorientating. "Unfortunately, ladies and gentlemen, due to the various mandates and regulations placed upon us by health and safety we have been denied permission to build a suitable pyre in the town square to ensure this witch is properly punished." He spoke with such a lightness of tone that some members of the crowd actually laughed, and there were a couple of joking cries of "Shame!"

"But other arrangements have been made," he continued. "As I am sure many of you are aware, one of the other methods of punishing a witch was to subject her to the humiliation of the ducking stool, and while we do not have exactly the device they would have used back then, we do have the means to lower our accused into a large quantity of water!"

The crowd parted for a third time as a large circular tank was pushed into the town square, covered with a thick tarpaulin.

Up high on her perch, still cold and scared, Lorraine had heard what the man had said and was almost at the point of crying tears of relief. It was all a show! Of course it was! And that man - she must have been mistaken! Besides, there was no way he could have been who she had thought he was. And now all they were going to do was dunk her in some water and let her go. She looked up at the sky. Thank God, she thought, and if I get out of here I promise I'm never going to gamble again. I'm going to go back to Peter and Davinia and be a proper mum and never cause my family any more trouble.

There was a creak. The ladder to which Lorraine was tied had been fixed at the lower end so that as the tension on the ropes holding the top end close to the pole was loosened, Lorraine was lowered face-first towards the ground, and towards the tank that had been positioned beneath her.

It's just water, she kept telling herself as the tarpaulin loomed nearer, it's just water and these loops aren't too tight. Once I'm down I'll be able to get out.

She was halfway towards it when the witchfinder pulled the tarpaulin away. Lorraine breathed another sigh of relief as she saw the water. She had been worried for a moment that it might be filled with something else - spikes or poisonous creatures.

It was only when she was very close that she noticed how the sunlight shimmered unnaturally on the liquid's surface, and that the lining of the tank seemed to be made of glass.

By then of course it was too late. The acid in the vat was so powerful that by the time it had eaten through her bonds it had already eaten through her face, and by the time anyone had managed to find something the acid didn't corrode to pull her out with, Lorraine Parsons was long gone.

And so was the witchfinder.

VIII

"So you're telling me that this man dissolved a girl in acid in front of forty witnesses and no-one can come up with a description of him?"

Longdon had known when the call came through that it was another one. After all, who else was going to be responsible for a hideous murder in a non-existent village filled with locals dressed as peasants and built by a hired-for-the-day crew who knew nothing more about the project than the numerous shell-shocked individuals they had interviewed so far?

"I think it's what he was wearing, sir," said Newham as the last of the ambulances took more than its safe quota of emotionally traumatised witnesses to the local hospital. "All they remember is the hat, the beard and that weird hairstyle he had."

"Which, according to that costume lady Melissa, is dead on mid seventeenth-century," said Longdon, frowning. "Did she seem a little bit odd to you?"

"They're film people, sir," said Newham. "They're all a bit odd."

"I suppose you're right," said Longdon as he glanced over to see two of his men getting dangerously close to the acid vat. "For God's sake, keep away from that until the disposal team arrives, can't you?" he shouted. "We've already got five members of the general public who need treating for acid burns. I don't want any of you lot turning up in their wake. It'll make us look even stupider than we already do."

"At least we've got an ID on the victim sir," said Newham, consulting her notebook. "Good thing that lawyer chap asked her what her name was."

Longdon nodded. It hadn't surprised him one little bit that it was another doctor. "How are we coming along with establishing a connection between these people?" he asked.

"Believe it or not, there are a number of links between the other three," said Jenny, flipping back a few pages. "The medical community's smaller than you think, and because of the way the training works, they'd all been around a whole load of different hospitals before settling down in their permanent jobs."

"Well, maybe this one will help us narrow it down. Even if we do we've still got four people dead and we're no closer to knowing what this lunatic might do next." Longdon rubbed his eyes.

"The smell of that tank getting to you, sir?" said Newham.

Longdon shook his head. "Been burning the midnight oil, Sergeant. I never thought I'd be subjecting myself to a non-stop diet of old horror films for the sake of a case but at the moment I have a stack of DVDs that reaches to the ceiling to get through."

Newham's phone bleeped and she flipped it open. "Well, at least we might be able to save you a few headaches," she said with a smile. "We've managed to dig up a local film critic who claims he knows all about the films of Vincent Price."

"Have you told him why we want to speak to him?" said Longdon as they headed for the car.

"No sir," said Newham. "I thought that would be best coming from you."

*

His name was Stanley Sanders. His hair was white, his velvet jacket was burgundy, and his age had to be well past bus pass qualification. He sat in Longdon's office with his hands clasped neatly on the desk as he was sworn to secrecy.

"It's vital for the case we're investigating at the moment, you see, sir," said Newham as she got him to sign all the appropriate forms.

"You mean the one that's all over the papers at the moment?" said Sanders in the kind of tired, aloof tones that made Longdon immediately feel sorry for any film-maker who had ended up under his critical eye. Jenny said that it was. "So you're asking me to keep quiet about what everyone in the country probably already knows?"

Longdon rolled his eyes. Why couldn't they have found some bright young thing who knew about this stuff? Preferably female, with a sunny disposition and a figure that could knock him into the middle of next week. He stopped his somewhat noirish daydreaming and regarded the slightly odd looking man in front of him.

"What we are about to tell you isn't common knowledge, sir," he explained. "And so far it's just theory. That's why we need your expert help."

"If you say so, Inspector," came the reply. "But I warn you now - my knowledge of film has lapsed somewhat since I left the paper. In fact I'd be hard pushed to remember anything past 1980."

Longdon frowned at Jenny, who shrugged. "I'm sure that will be fine, sir." He proceeded to explain the events in the case so far. Sanders looked alternately shocked, intrigued and impressed as Longdon listed the deaths and the suspected inspiration behind them. Eventually he came to the latest, which he described in the kind of detail that had Mr Sanders reaching for the scented handkerchief in his pocket.

"That'll be Witchfinder General, then," said the ex-movie critic with a cough. "Quite a classic if I say so myself. The scene he's decided to reproduce is the one where Vincent Price, playing Matthew Hopkins, engineers the death of one of the accused village girls by a method that is probably completely historically inaccurate but which certainly made for a dramatic scene in the movie. Of course, your girl was dissolved in acid, which might also be a nod to 1953's House of Wax, or possibly Scream and Scream Again, made fourteen years later."

"That's all very helpful, sir," said Longdon. "But what we really need to know is - how many films are there where Vincent Price kills people?"

There was a pause while Sanders counted on his fingers, paused, shook his head, started counting again and then eventually said, "I'm not sure - maybe thirty or so?" As Longdon and his sergeant looked horrified he added, "but of course that's not including the films in which Vincent Price stars and people are killed by people other than him, such as your first murder. If it's based on the one from Corman's Masque of the Red Death, Vincent Price doesn't actually do the killing in that particular instance."

Longdon soon began to regret asking Stanley to go on as what he had anticipated as a short chat began to evolve into a two hour lecture on horror films. Eventually he was relieved when the Chief Inspector rang, which was something he never thought he would find himself admitting to. He picked up the receiver and consulted his notes while Jenny escorted Stanley out.

"Yes sir," he said, doing his best to placate his already irritated-sounding senior officer, "we do seem to be fairly sure that it's the same killer in each of these cases." He winced at the next question. "No sir, I'm afraid we aren't any closer to identifying him." He looked at the notes he had made while Stanley had been talking. "We're working on the theory that whoever he is he's been setting this up for years. The name of the man who had the affair with Mrs Pritchard, the real name of Captain Clowney, and the name of the individual who hired everyone for the reality film shoot we have noted down as Henry Jarrod, Anton Phibes and Edward Lionheart respectively, all of whom I am now reliably informed are characters played in films by the actor Vincent Price." He paused to allow the Chief Inspector to speak. "That's right sir - Vincent Price. An actor, sir, in horror films. Old ones. Apparently the deaths all mimic his films, too. Yes, I know it sounds very far-fetched, sir. Yes sir, absolutely ridiculous - I agree, sir. But to be honest, it's the only lead we have, and according to our expert. A local film critic, sir. It just seemed to be a good idea to..." Longdon realised there was little point in continuing as the voice on the other end of the line became a tirade. Sergeant Newham walked back in just as Longdon was putting down the receiver.

"Bad news, sir?" she asked

"Well, his Lordship isn't happy," said Longdon, "and I can't say I blame him. Four deaths and the only thing linking them a bunch of films they don't even show on late night television any more." He pointed at his hastily scribbled notes. "Do you know how many films there are where Vincent Price murders someone?" Jenny shook her head. "Thirty. And there's usually more than one murder per film." He put his head in his hands. "God knows how many more there are going to be before this is finished."

"Probably five more at the most, sir," said Jenny, passing him the piece of paper she had brought in. Longdon rubbed his eyes and stared at the paper. "It's the link we've been looking for," she continued. "Putting Lorraine Parsons into the equation clinched it but it took me a while to check all the facts. And type it out so it was easy for you to read."

Longdon ignored her smile as he looked at the name at the top of the page.

"Victoria Valentine," he read.

Jenny nodded. "They were all involved in her case. She was an eleven-year- old girl dragged out of the river following a car accident. She was close to death when they brought her to the hospital and as far as I can tell it was a hopeless case even though they all did their best - casualty officers, surgical team, anaesthetists - apparently one of them was a GP who happened to be at the scene of the accident. Of course most of them were junior staff who moved and ended up training in different specialties, but that's the only case that links the victims."

Longdon read through the list of names. “So that leaves us with Christopher Skilbeck, Jasper Morgan, David Sparkes, Geoffrey Marsden and Caroline Conrad.”

Jenny frowned, took the list off him and looked at it again. “Sorry, sir, my mistake,” she said as she handed it back. “I said there might be five more potential victims but in fact there are only four. Dr Conrad died last year. Misadventure.”

Longdon raised an eyebrow. “Nothing suspicious, then?”

“Well, now that you mention it...” The sergeant looked uneasy. “She was a nerve specialist and had been plagued for years herself with chronic back pain. In fact, she’d volunteered to be a guinea pig for some kind of electronic spinal implant. Anyway, when they found her it had somehow malfunctioned and she’d received a massive electric shock to her spine.”

Longdon groaned. “Oh God, it’s The Tingler.”

“The verdict was that she must have somehow tried to boost the signal from the implant and ended up killing herself.”

“No,” said Longdon, “it’s The Tingler. Vincent Price discovers this creature that can crush your spine when you’re afraid. According to our Mr Sanders you had to scream to dislodge it. I don’t supposed she was gagged when they found her?”

Jenny shrugged. “No idea, sir. Shall I find out?”

Longdon shook his head. “No, never mind. I think we can safely up the body count to five. All we’re missing is a suspect. What about the family of this little girl?”

“Well that’s where it gets interesting,” said Jenny.

“Oh good,” said Longdon as sarcastically as he could manage. “This has been such a dull case so far.”

“The man driving the car was Edward Valentine, who was the chief surgeon at the hospital they took her to. He knew all the staff who treated her. Well, he would have known them.”

“What do you mean?”

“Edward Valentine’s body was never found,” said Jenny. “It was assumed he drowned in the wreck and his body was washed out to sea. We’re very close to the Bristol Channel here, sir.”

“I am aware of that, sergeant,” he said irritably, “living in Bristol and everything.”

“Sorry, sir. Anyway, they never found him and there was no other family. It was all very sad, actually.”

"And the story's not exactly getting any brighter, is it?" said Longdon, handing the sheet back to her. "Get every one of these people on the 'phone, tell them their lives are quite probably in danger, and that we are making arrangements for them to be taken to a safe house until we find out who's doing this."

"Already taken care of, sir," the sergeant replied. "Where exactly are we going to take them?"

"No bloody idea at the moment," said Longdon. "But well done for sorting all that."

Jenny smiled. "You were talking to Mr Sanders for quite a long time."

"I bloody was as well," said Longdon, looking at his pencilled scribblings. "By the way," he said. "Do any of these men keep poodles?"

Jenny looked confused. "No sir, why?"

"Oh, just something Mr Sanders mentioned," said Longdon with a shudder. "So have we had any responses yet?"

"The only one we know anything about is Dr Sparkes, who's on holiday in the South of France."

Longdon breathed a sigh of relief. "Well he should be safe enough down there," he said.

"I'm not sure, sir," said Jenny. "Apparently he was meant to be back at work a week ago. He hasn't been seen since he set off for a tour of the wine-producing areas."

Longdon's face fell in resignation. "So he's probably nailed inside a barrel somewhere, then," he said.

"Sir?"

Longdon tapped his notes. "Tower of London - a remake, apparently. Or possibly Theatre of Blood. Either way it's all to do with Richard III bumping off the Duke of Clarence by drowning him in a vat of wine."

"Well, I suppose we could keep our fingers crossed that he's just lost," she said as she went back to the list. "Otherwise we've left messages with Dr Skilbeck and Mr Marsden, who was the surgeon in charge of the case. Mrs Morgan told us that her husband Jasper retired a year ago and now spends much of his time wandering around the country putting together a book on old churches, which is what he's doing at the moment."

"Any idea where he might be?"

"Somewhere in Wales I think, sir, but exactly where not even his wife knows."

Longdon stared at the list of films before him, filled with murder, mutilation and suffering. Surely whoever was doing this wouldn't have the nerve to kill someone in a church, would they?

"In that case, Sergeant, as you so aptly put it, let's keep our fingers crossed that he's all right."

IX

"How simply marvellous!"

Jasper Morgan clapped his hands and crowed with delight as he regarded the stained glass design in the church's east window. How unexpected to find such a beautiful rendition in such an out of the way spot!

"It is a very good example of its type, isn't it?" said the vicar. "We're so proud of it here that it's always a pleasure to be able to 'show it off' as it were, especially to someone who knows a little about these matters. Such individuals are, I can assure you, few and far between."

Morgan nodded with enthusiasm before turning round to behold the rest of the church of St Valentine. "I must admit I'd been hoping I might be allowed a private personal tour of this particular building," he said, "but, in all confidence, my dear fellow, I had heard from some of the locals that the vicar wasn't the most co-operative of sorts!"

The vicar gave him an extra-wide smile. "They may well have been referring to the last curate of this parish," he said. "I've only just very recently arrived, and when I learned of your visiting the area it seemed somehow appropriate that you should be the first to receive a guided tour from my good self."

"Appropriate?" Morgan frowned as the vicar put his arm around his shoulders and led him down the aisle.

"Why, yes, indeed," the vicar continued. "My dear chap, an enthusiast for church design who, in his autumn years, is thinking of devoting some of his well- earned retirement to the composition of a tome on the very subject? What more appropriate an individual could there be?"

They had reached the end of the aisle. Morgan was about to examine the font when he felt himself being turned round.

"You can get a much better view of the window from back here," the vicar said.

It was true. From here, with the afternoon sunlight filtering through the greens and reds, it was possible to behold the true majesty in the depiction of Saint Valentine performing the act that had apparently led to his sanctification.

"You know what he's doing to the little girl?"

Morgan glanced at his companion and then back to the glass. "I remember reading it somewhere," he said, hesitating, "but I'd appreciate it if you could refresh my memory."

"Of course," said the vicar. He pointed to the kneeling child. "The story goes that Valentine, while under house arrest, was asked to cure the sight of the judge's blind daughter, which he duly did, resulting in the conversion of much of the judge's household to the faith." He sighed. "It must have been wonderful to have been able to save a little girl like that. Our Lord does move in mysterious ways. Of course," he continued with a little laugh, "it did often end quite badly for His servants. I believe Saint Valentine suffered a fate considered at the time to be an appropriate punishment for his alleged 'miracle'."

The vicar looked at Morgan as if prompting him. All Jasper could do was nod and reply, "Of course, of course."

"I hope you would not consider it too forward of me if I were to perhaps remind you of that as well?" said the vicar after allowing a suitable period of time to pass during which Dr Morgan resolutely failed to provide the information himself.

"Please do," said the doctor. He had produced a small notebook from his knapsack and was now taking out a pencil. The vicar left him to his scribbling and proceeded back up the aisle.

"Some stories say that he was stabbed to death by a drunken mob, others that he was run through with a spear and then dragged through the streets tied to the tail of a horse."

"Tail...of...a...horse," Morgan mouthed the words as he wrote them down while the vicar allowed him to catch up.

"Oh yes. Then there is the story of his being beheaded. I believe they used to do that to quite a lot of saints."

"It did rather put a stop to what they were up to, didn't it?" said Morgan with a childlike chuckle.

"I suppose so," said the vicar, nearing the choir stalls. "As far as I am aware there are, however, no stories of his being drowned, burned alive, or being force fed his own children." He stepped behind the pulpit, and disappeared.

"Did they really do that?" said Morgan, looking aghast.

The vicar's voice carried on from where he was momentarily hidden. "Oh, you wouldn't believe some of the punishments that have been meted out to the guilty over the years, Dr Morgan, you really wouldn't.

Anyway, I am reliably informed that the true means of St Valentine's martyrdom was by a device similar to this one here."

With that the vicar returned, wheeling a complicated-looking contraption into the aisle. It consisted of a metal framework on four wheels, from the top of which protruded two long runners that extended far beyond the device itself.

"What on earth is that?" said Morgan, fascinated. He tucked away his notebook and rushed forward to examine it.

"Medieval technology," said the vicar with a grin. "Don't touch it - it's very old, and very fragile. Of course there's no way of proving that this is the actual device that was used and I very much doubt it was, but it certainly dates from the time and -" here he gave Morgan a big smile "- it is fun to pretend."

"Oh yes it is!" said the doctor, taking out his camera. He was about to press the button and then stopped. "I presume it's all right if I..."

The vicar nodded. "Of course, my dear fellow, of course! Take as many pictures as you like, and of the window as well if you wish."

Dr Morgan was allowed his amusement for ten minutes before he was interrupted.

"Do you know," said the vicar, "I've just had an idea."

"What's that, then?" said Morgan, now back down at the atrium and taking pictures of the frankly uninteresting font.

"What if I were to take a picture of you pretending to succumb to this old thing here?" The vicar gave the framework a very gentle pat. "So you could be seen to be suffering the martyrdom of St Valentine - in the Church of St Valentine?"

The doctor's glee at the idea was almost matched by his companion's. "I say, would you? I mean, would you mind?"

"Well, it's not every day we have someone like you in here so I don't see why we shouldn't make a special effort," the vicar replied, looking around him. "Now, we need something for you to sit in." His eyes roamed the church for a moment before settling on an ornate-looking chair near the choir stalls. "That should do nicely," he said.

He picked the chair up and set it carefully at the head of the aisle, facing away from the altar. "This is where the bishop sits when he comes to offer his benediction," he said, lowering his voice to a whisper. "But if you promise not to tell anyone, then neither will I."

Morgan was barely able to contain his excitement. "Cross my heart and hope to die," he said.

"Indeed," said the vicar, adjusting the cushion before Morgan sat down. "Now, Saint Valentine would of course have been restrained," his eyes began to search the building again.

"What about those pretend manacles over there?" Morgan said, pointing to a nearby anti-slavery exhibition that had apparently been put together by a local school. A set of rusty-looking chains hung next to brightly illustrated poems about torture and repression.

"Well spotted!" The vicar crossed the aisle and picked them up. They rattled as he did so. "Looks like someone managed to find the real thing," he said. "They're a bit dusty - I hope that's not going to be a problem?"

"Not at all," said Morgan. "It'll add to the authenticity, and that will add to the chances of my book selling."

"Of course," said the vicar, clamping Morgan's wrists to the arms of the chair. The key was even rustier, and grated in the locks as he turned it. "Comfy?"

"It's a bit tight," the doctor replied, "but that's okay. It's only for a moment, after all."

"We need to keep your head still as well," said his companion. "Partly for authenticity but mostly for your own safety." He attached a leather strap that ran under Morgan's chin and behind his ears. It achieved the job admirably. "And now we're almost ready to begin!"

The vicar wheeled the device round so that it was facing the now helpless doctor and proceeded to arrange the runners so that they were propped either side of his head. "And can you guess what goes on here?" he asked.

Morgan would have shaken his head if he'd been able to. Instead he croaked a muffled "No."

The vicar reached behind the near-most pew and picked up a tiny trolley to which had been affixed two steel daggers. He placed the little vehicle on the runners and ran it back as far away from Morgan as the metal rails would allow.

"Ideally they should be red hot," he said as he attached the trolley bearing the blades to a heavy spring at the end of the frame, "but we can't have everything. Now, what should actually happen is this: the little trolley is released and it runs along these rails, and then the knives put out your eyes."

"Put out my eyes?" mumbled Jasper.

"Exactly," the vicar nodded, "and not just that. The force imparted to the blades by the spring at the back here means that in actuality they wouldn't just blind you; they would be driven through the back of your skull and into the chair itself."

"The bishop wouldn't be pleased," said Morgan, trying to laugh. "And that's how St Valentine was martyred, is it?"

The vicar's expression changed as he came closer and leaned over the helpless doctor. "No," he said. "Not at all, actually."

The doctor eyed the steel spring-loaded knife blades and then looked back at the vicar. "I beg your pardon?"

"You know, I really must give you credit for living up - or rather, down - to my expectations, Jasper," said the black clad figure, much more coldly now. "I suspected you would be as lazy and incompetent a researcher of church history as you were an anaesthetist, and it would seem I have been proven correct."

"What on earth do you mean?" Morgan coughed against the neck restraint and tried to struggle, but it was too tight.

"I mean that you have no idea who St Valentine was, do you? Just like in the old days, you intended to rely on someone else telling you all you needed to know so you could struggle on without actually having the faintest clue what you were doing. Well, this time, that has backfired." Now there was barely concealed anger in his tone. As he leaned close to his prisoner his voice was barely a whisper. "You don't recognise me, do you?"

The doctor tried to shake his head.

"No," said the vicar, removing his upper row of fake teeth. "It's amazing what a false overbite, a pair of glasses, and of course ten years of utter agony can do to alter the appearance of someone you used to know so well."

The penny had dropped now. Morgan stared in shock as he mouthed his captor's name.

"Yes," said the man who had imprisoned him, "It's me. It is Edward Valentine, returned from the grave to claim his just revenge. Tell me - have you ever seen a film called Theatre of Blood?" Morgan shook his head. "That's a pity. It's a very good film. Of course you're not going to get the chance to see it now, or anything else for that matter. So I suppose it's just as well that I summarised every one of its quite outrageous and horrible murders as part of that poppycock I was making up about the fate of that poor saint." He paused, returning to the device he had attached to Morgan's chair. "Every murder except one, that is." He stroked the button that would release the spring. "You're about to be blinded, Dr Morgan, but before I release the knives I feel I ought to tell you that you're not the first to receive such a dramatic method of punishment. I do, however, feel that you are the one that's most going to upset the christening that's due in here in about half an hour."

"For God's sake, Valentine!" Morgan pleaded, trying hard to turn his face away from the trajectory of the shining steel. "There was no way we could save her! We all tried! We all did our best! It was a hopeless case! Please! Please! For God's sake!"

"Not for God's sake, Dr Morgan," said the man in black. "For mine."

His thumb came down on the button.

X

"And that is why there are only two of you left."

Longdon regarded the shocked expressions of the two men sitting in front of him in the station's interview room. It had been the only place available for him to talk to them when they had been brought in, and their concern that they had both been apprehended regarding some unknown misdemeanour had quickly turned to horror as Longdon recounted the series of deaths that had occurred over the last few days.

"And are you seriously suggesting that Edward Valentine is responsible for all of this?" Geoffrey Marsden must have been close to sixty but he wore it well. The few streaks of grey in his hair matched his eyes, and while he was obviously shaken, his stoic expression betrayed the fact that he had witnessed horror many times during his long career.

"We think so, sir," said Longdon. "For a start, Dr Valentine's body was never found. Second, it's impossible to think of anyone else who could bear such a grudge against such a disparate group of people."

"If what you say is true, then why haven't you caught him yet?" demanded Christopher Skilbeck. He had been Marsden's junior ten years ago but was now a consultant surgeon himself and had been dragged down from Nottingham. The rotund little man was sweating and his black suit looked rumpled.

"Well, for a start, the only pictures we have of him are ten years old," said Longdon. "Plus, he seems to have managed to get close enough to his victims without them recognising him that we suspect his appearance has either radically altered, or he has become something of a master of disguise."

"Either that or they just weren't expecting someone long dead to turn up and try to kill them," said Marsden. "At least we're forewarned."

"And under protection, sir," said Longdon. "Until all of this has blown over."

"What does that mean?" Skilbeck fidgeted in his chair. "I've got patients to see."

"We appreciate that you both have, sir." said Longdon, "but neither of you are going to be of much use to your patients dead, so if you'll just bear with us, then hopefully we can prevent that from happening."

There was a pause as that sank in.

"How exactly do you propose to prevent us from being killed?" said Marsden. "We aren't going to have to go to some dreadful safe house are we?" Both he and Skilbeck paled at the mention of the word.

"All our safe houses are full at the moment, sir," said Longdon, their disdain not lost on him. "So our only alternative was to keep you in the cells here." He paused again for effect and for the joy of seeing their faces. "But fortunately one of our staff has volunteered his own home." He held up his hands. "Now, before you start complaining I should explain that it's Dr Richard Patterson, our pathologist, and the only reason I've agreed is that apparently he's got some huge old rambling place in the country south of here, so there should be plenty of room and little chance that anyone should be able to find out where you are. As well as that, you'll both be assigned police protection."

"Where is this place?" said Skilbeck.

"Probably best if you don't know the details, sir," said Longdon. "One text message to a wife or a mistress and for all we know our Dr Valentine will have picked it up and will be on his way there."

"And even with police protection you think he's still a threat to us?" said Marsden.

Longdon leaned over the table separating him from the two men. "Have you not been listening to what I've been saying? This is a man who has managed to get a man stung to death by scorpions in front of a room full of children. Who has put together an entire seventeenth-century village filled with volunteers in front of whom he then dissolved a woman in acid. In the last seven days he has flung someone off the Clifton Suspension Bridge, impaled someone on the roof of the Bristol Council House, and popped over to Wales to spear one of your former anaesthetic colleagues through his eye sockets while he sat manacled to a bishop's chair. So in answer to your question: yes - no matter what we do, I will still very much consider this man to be a threat."

Marsden and Skilbeck exchanged fearful glances.

"Well if you put it like that..." said Marsden, shifting in his seat.

"I do," said Longdon as Jenny Newham entered the room. "Now, if you would both be good enough to go with the sergeant, she will arrange transport for you. Your families have already been informed of the situation and they know you are under our protection, so you needn't worry."

The two men waited in the corridor while Longdon gave Jenny some final instructions.

"And if you see Richard, tell him thank you, will you?" he said.

"Well, when I last saw him I got the impression you didn't give him much choice," said Jenny with a grin.

"That's his own bloody fault for offering in the first place. I know he just wanted to brag about having a big house and he never thought we'd take him up on it, but that's his problem." Longdon got out of the chair and stretched. "Who've we got assigned to protect Lord and Lady Precious out there?"

Jenny pretended to think for a moment. "We've got Shenley and Standen there until 10.30 this evening, then I think you'll find it's you and me."

"Always drawing the short bloody straw," said Longdon with a sigh.

"Is that you or me, sir?" said Jenny as he followed her out.

"Now, you start being cheeky and you might find yourself reassigned to something a bit less glamorous," said Longdon with a smile. "I'll see you tonight. When absolutely nothing is going to happen, right?"

Jenny gave him the firmest of nods. "Right."

They were, of course, to be proved wrong.

XI

Patterson's house was hidden deep within the wilds of Somerset. Despite that, and an evening that kept threatening rain, Jenny Newham was only five minutes late for her shift. She parked her blue Mini in front of the rambling gothic building, which was nothing more than a black silhouette against the charcoal clouds gathering overhead, and knocked as hard as she could on the heavy oak door.

It was opened almost immediately by a man she recognised as DS Michael Shenley. A grin crossed his freckled face as he realised who it was.

"So," he said, "you found it, then?"

Jenny returned his smile as she went inside. "It was a bit of a maze getting here," she said. "Thank God for sat nav."

If the outside of the building had been imposing, the inside was almost overwhelming. A huge entrance hall boasted an ornate staircase running up the left-hand wall and leading to the upper floor. The rest of the wall space was taken up with suits of armour, antique swords, and other items of medieval weaponry. A door to the right led into the lounge.

"Do you think Patterson caught this himself?" Jenny tapped the stuffed grizzly bear that was positioned near the front door. It didn't growl and instead made a rather hollow sound.

"No idea," said Shenley. "But we haven't seen him this evening. Otherwise I would have asked him. He rang earlier, though. Apparently he's stuck doing a couple of post-mortems, otherwise he'd be here."

"Not more victims?" said Jenny.

Shenley shook his head. "Nothing to do with this case as far as I'm aware." He glanced upstairs. "Our two little boys are sleeping like babies."

Jenny snorted. "It's a bit early for bedtime, isn't it? What have they been doing?"

Shenley led her into the vast room to the right, where on a table near the huge bay window were lying two empty bottles of J&B whiskey and two glasses. "The same thing doctors always do when they get bored," he said, pointing at the detritus that had been left by Messrs

Marsden and Skilbeck. "I'm not sure how happy Patterson's going to be about them raiding his drinks cabinet."

Jenny looked around the room, marvelling at the huge open fireplace opposite the door, the rich fabric of the curtains that hung over the windows both front and rear, and the book-lined walls. "He's pretty comfortable in here, isn't he?"

"We haven't had much of a chance to look round," said a voice from the door.

Jenny turned to see the wiry figure of DS Vince Standen. "We've been too busy looking after our increasingly pissed-up charges," he said, "at least until a couple of hours ago when they finally dragged themselves off upstairs. Since then we've been alternating patrolling the grounds and checking all the doors and windows."

"It's been all quiet," said Shenley, handing her the paperwork and making to leave. "Hope your night's the same." He paused by the lounge door. "Where's your colleague, by the way?"

"Oh, he's more lost than I was," said Jenny with a grin. "I called him on the radio before I came inside. He should be here in about half an hour."

"Well, if you're sure?" Shenley gave her a look of concern.

"I'll be fine," she replied, taking out her gun and waving it, "and besides, they've given me this awful thing to help defend myself with. Now off you go."

The first thing Jenny did once they were gone was tidy up the whiskey bottles. She wouldn't have been able to help herself anyway, but the thought of Richard Patterson turning up and going crazy about his plundered alcohol supply meant that hopefully she had managed to avert at least one crisis this evening.

Next, she went to check on her charges.

The staircase was carpeted in thick scarlet-coloured pile and Jenny's boots made no sound on the thick fabric as she made her way upstairs, past paintings of people who didn't resemble her pathologist colleague in the slightest. She made a mental note to ask him about them when he finally turned up.

A walnut-panelled corridor led away from the landing, with rooms either side. The first one was lushly furnished but unoccupied. The second revealed the heavily sleeping form of one of her charges. His black hair identified him as Christopher Skilbeck, as did the fairly capacious clothes that had been strewn across the intricately woven Persian carpet.

Next door was much the same, only here the heavily sedated individual hidden beneath the sheets had streaks of grey in his hair, and a tweed jacket that had been clumsily hung on a bedpost before Geoffrey Marsden had retired for the evening. Jenny shut the door behind her. There was one other room on the corridor, which Jenny checked for security. This was also unoccupied and was presumably used by Patterson as a viewing room, as the only items of furniture were an ornately carved straight-backed chair which was positioned four feet before the widescreen television set that took up the entire left-hand corner. Both the screen and the room were currently in darkness. Jenny crossed the room and drew back the curtains to make a cursory inspection of the window, which had been bolted shut. It must have been a trick of the light, because as she looked through the glass at the countryside beyond, it almost looked as if there were bars on the outside.

She was on her way back downstairs when the front door opened. She smiled, expecting to see Longdon, and her face fell when she realised it wasn't him.

"I very much hope that face isn't for me!" said Patterson, shrugging off his overcoat and hanging it on the grizzly's muzzle.

Jenny apologised. "It's just I was expecting it to be DI Longdon," she explained. "He still isn't here yet."

"Probably got lost," said Patterson going into the lounge and rubbing his hands. "The roads around here can be a bit interminable. Would you like a drink?"

"Not while I'm on duty," she reminded him.

"No, no, of course not. Silly of me." Patterson went to the Victorian-looking globe by the window and flipped up the lid to reveal his drinks cabinet. He eyed it with disbelief. "Have they really drunk all of my scotch?" he said.

Jenny shrugged. "Apparently so," she said.

"Bloody surgeons," said Patterson, pouring himself a gin from a nearly full bottle of Hendricks and squirting in a few drops of tonic. He paused before taking a mouthful. "Can I get you something else? Tea or coffee?"

"Maybe later - thanks," said Jenny as the pathologist took another sip from the glass.

"Very well, but do let me know if you get thirsty," he said. "How are our guests doing? Have you had a look at them yet?"

"Sleeping soundly," Jenny replied. "I don't think we're going to hear a peep out of them all night."

"Good stuff," Patterson took another sip. "So all we have to worry about is our Dr Valentine getting in here and murdering us in some ludicrous and unimaginable way."

"Not us," said Jenny, "them. He's only bumping off the people he wants revenge on."

"Yes, of course," said Patterson, putting the glass down. "Well, if you'll excuse me I have a few things to do before I turn in. You're sure I can't get you anything?"

Jenny shook her head. "I'll be fine, thanks. I'll just wait here until Longdon arrives."

"Very well," he said with a smile. "Don't be alarmed by any banging around you hear upstairs - it'll just be me."

"I'll check anyway if you don't mind," said Jenny. "Any banging around might just be our suspect killing the men we're supposed to be protecting, and that wouldn't look good for anyone."

"You've got a point there," said Patterson, making for the stairs. "Maybe I'll bump into you in a bit."

Jenny smiled and checked her watch. Longdon should have been here by now. Presumably he was still stuck on the back roads of Somerset somewhere. She closed the drinks cabinet lid and then looked around the room. She'd already checked upstairs, and Patterson would raise the alarm if anything happened up there now, so in order to keep herself busy she decided to check the outside of the house.

She was careful to leave the door on the latch and took the torch from the boot of her car. The wind was picking up as Jenny made her way back to the front of the house and proceeded to make a circuit of the outside of the building. The windows at the back were securely shut.

As Jenny tugged on the back door handle she felt a slight spatter of rain, accompanied by a flash of lightning. She waited for the inevitable thunder clap that would follow so she could get an idea of how far away the storm might be, but none came. A few more drops of rain fell, followed by another flash of white light, and this time Jenny realised that the light wasn't due to an electric storm at all.

It was coming from one of the upstairs windows.

By the time she had made her way back round to the front of the house, Jenny had worked out that the light was coming from the empty room that she had last looked in - the one with nothing in it but the TV. Patterson was probably watching something before going to bed, but she knew she needed to check on it anyway.

When she got back inside the house the lights were off.

Jenny flicked the switch by the door but nothing happened. Great, she thought, a power failure on a night like tonight. She used the torch beam to find the stairs and climbed halfway up before calling out.

"Dr Patterson? Are you all right up there?"

There was no reply.

"Richard?" Jenny began to climb the stairs once more, but more cautiously now. The flickering white light came again, this time from the landing. Everything was just suspicious enough that by the time she reached the first floor Jenny had decided she was going to have to wake up the two men she had been sent there to protect, regardless of how drunk or hungover they might be.

The flickering light was coming from the room at the far end. The door was only open a fraction, but the rest of the house was in such darkness that the light was conspicuous. Jenny called Patterson's name again and when yet again there was no reply, she knocked on the door to Christopher Skilbeck's room and went in.

The surgeon was still asleep, the glow from Jenny's torch picking out his motionless form beneath the blankets. Jenny coughed loudly to try to wake him, even though she knew it was unlikely he would hear her.

"Mr. Skilbeck?" she said, coming closer. "Mr Skilbeck, I'm sorry to have to disturb you but for safety's sake it's probably best if we have you awake just for now."

The figure in the bed did not move.

Jenny was almost over him now, and as the torch beam played over his body Jenny thought he was breathing remarkably lightly for a man drunk to the point of being comatose. In fact it didn't look as if he was breathing at all.

"Sir?" Jenny reached out a hand to shake the man's shoulder. Nothing. "Mr Skilbeck," she said, pulling back the blankets, "I'm sorry about this but I'm going to have to--"

She was cut off in mid sentence by what she saw beneath the bedsheet. Christopher Skilbeck's head was lying on the white pillow, but the body below it was all wrong. It was too thin and too tall to be that of the man she had seen in Longdon's office.

Then she saw the pool of blood where Skilbeck's head had been surgically stitched to the other body's neck.

Jenny stifled a scream and threw back the covers completely. In the swaying beam of the torch held in her shaking hand she saw that the head and right arm of Mr Christopher Skilbeck had been stitched to what looked like the body of Mr Geoffrey Marsden.

Jenny spun round and flashed the torch around the room. She released the breath she had been holding when she was satisfied that there was no-one else in there with her. Then, as quietly as she could, she tiptoed next door, where she found Mr Marsden's missing head and arm had been stitched onto the squatter torso of Mr Skilbeck in the same way.

The killer wasn't here, either.

A muffled cry came from the room at the end of the corridor; the one with the flickering light. Jenny drew her gun and called out.

"Police! I'm warning you now - I'm armed and there's backup on the way. The best thing you can do now is give yourself up."

Silence.

"Richard," she said, "are you okay?"

Still silence.

Again Jenny thought about going back downstairs to radio for backup, but her overriding concern was that Patterson might have caught Valentine in the act. He might be in that room now, being subjected to some form of hideous electric shock treatment that was killing him while she was standing here dithering.

Her mind made up, she crept up to the door of the last room on the right and nudged it open.

The television was on.

She didn't really register what was playing on the screen. It looked like some film about medieval times, with the villain having trapped the helpless hero beneath some huge swinging torture instrument that was threatening to cut him in half. That was all she saw before her attention was drawn to the chair.

Someone was sitting in it.

No, some thing was sitting in it.

The tiny, still figure was no bigger than a child, and as Jenny crept closer she realised that was what it was. A little girl, pigtails tied with blue ribbon, brightly polished shoes on feet that couldn't quite reach the floor. As good as gold and as still as the grave, sitting patiently while the film on the television screen came to an end.

Jenny checked there was no-one behind her, and then spoke.

"I don't want to scare you," she said. "But my name's Jenny and I'm a police officer. I need you to come with me."

As she reached the chair Jenny felt her legs turn to water as she realised her words were falling on deaf ears. Dead ears, in fact. As dead as the rest of the beautifully dressed, well preserved, mummified corpse of a little girl that had been propped up in the chair to watch a film on which the credits were now rolling and which starred...

"Vincent Price, of course," said a cold voice from behind her.

Jenny Newham turned to see a figure silhouetted in the open doorway. As it took a step forward she realised who it was. And she also suddenly understood why it had been arranged for the last two victims to come here.

"You're not Dr Patterson at all, are you?" she said, pointing the gun at the man who seemed to have grown several inches taller since she had last seen him.

"On the contrary, my dear young lady, I am," he replied, taking another step into the room, "or at least I have been for the last ten years. The man who was Richard Patterson before that suffered a rather unfortunate accident that left his place on a training scheme in forensic pathology free. But yes, before that I was, and indeed still am, Dr Edward Valentine. Or rather, Mr. Edward Valentine, at your service."

He gave a little bow while keeping his eyes on the gun.

Jenny glanced at the thing in the chair. "Then that... that... child is..."

"Victoria?" Now Valentine was looking over Jenny's shoulder and addressing the corpse of the child directly. "Has the film finished?" He looked back at Jenny. "The Pit and the Pendulum is one of her favourites, you know. In fact, I believe I told Detective Inspector Longdon that at one point. You know, I can't tell you how many times we watched some of these before... " His voice tailed off as he looked behind Jenny again. "If the film's finished then it's bedtime, as well you know," he said to the withered lifeless figure in the chair. "You won't object if I put her to bed, will you?" Now he was addressing Jenny again. "It's just that she does get a little grumpy if I let her stay up too late."

Jenny trained the gun on him. "You're under arrest, Dr Valentine," she said, "and you're going to come downstairs with me where we're both going to wait until DI Longdon gets here."

"Oh, I don't think he'll be here for some time," said Valentine with a chuckle. "The directions I gave him should have taken him a good twenty miles in the opposite direction, and I do so hope he resorts to his sat nav so the false postcode I gave him can be put to good use. I'm sure he'll get here eventually -" and now his voice was cold again "- but before he does I have plans for you, young lady. You don't really think I had only just arrived home when I pretended to, do you?" He gave Jenny a wicked smile and then looked behind her once again. "Victoria, stop that!"

This last sentence was barked out loudly and so abruptly that Jenny couldn't help glancing behind her. That was all the time Valentine needed to wrest the gun from her and clamp the chloroform-soaked cloth over her mouth and nose. She fought for only a few seconds before darkness descended.

XII

It was close to midnight when Longdon finally got to Patterson's house, his sat nav switched off and his temper frayed after having got directions from a pub on the verge of a lock-in over in Clevedon. The petrified-looking landlord had relaxed a little, and become far more co-operative, once Longdon had explained that the police business he was on was not the closing down of small rural public houses. In fact, once Longdon had ordered a pint and one for the landlord as well, the man had gone so far as to draw a map to Patterson's house.

"At least I think that's where you want to go, sir," he said, scratching his stubbly jowls. "It's the only place around here that fits that description. Mind you, even if it is owned by a doctor, that still don't rightly explain the weird building jobs they've had over there the last couple of months."

Longdon didn't really have time for chit-chat but something in the publican's tone made him want to know more. "How on earth would you know?" he asked.

"Small part of the world, sir," came the reply. "We all know each other's business around here."

Longdon nodded. That part was true enough. "What kind of building jobs?" he asked.

The landlord looked around and then became more conspiratorial. "Well, it's all a bit strange, sir, if you ask me. My wife's second cousin, Les, well he had to deliver all this metalwork that he said looked as if it would be more at home in some kind of ancient museum."

Longdon's interest dropped. So that was all the man meant. "You mean suits of armour, swords, that kind of thing?"

The landlord nodded. "But that's not all. He had to pick something up from the Avonmouth ferry. Came over from Spain apparently." The man leaned in closer and Longdon was surprised he couldn't smell booze. "He says it was the biggest blade he'd ever seen, shaped like a crescent moon and of a size that could cut a man in half." Suddenly he seemed embarrassed by his outburst. "Well," he said, more soberly, "it could if it was connected up to all the other stuff he picked up as well. Like some huge pendulum, apparently."

Longdon was out the door and into his car before the landlord even realised he had gone. As he crossed beneath the motorway, stopping regularly to examine the pencil-drawn map, Longdon was scarcely able to believe what his instincts were telling him. Patterson had been with them for years. But not more than ten years, he reminded himself, in fact only just less than five. Where had he been before that? Had the man who had performed all the post-mortems actually killed people himself, even Dr Richard Patterson, or had he somehow assumed the man's identity at some point before coming to Bristol? Even with the stringent checks available, Longdon knew all too well how easy it was to falsify paperwork, forge certificates and, if one so wished, take on another identity entirely. All you needed to be was resourceful, wealthy, and very, very clever. Dr Edward Valentine had been all three. And, thought Longdon with a shiver as he drove as fast as he could down the pitch-dark country roads, he probably still was.

*

The house was in darkness when Longdon arrived. Hammering on the front door yielded nothing in the way of a response, and the heavy oak was too robust to force, so instead Longdon resorted to an inspection of the ground floor windows. The front of the house appeared impregnable. It was when he went round the back that he saw, about thirty feet away from the main building, set back in the house's capacious grounds, what looked like a stone temple.

A stone temple with light seeping from beneath its double doors.

Longdon took one final look at the house before deciding that if he was going to get any answers and, indeed, save any lives tonight, it was probably going to be over there.

The ground was soft underfoot and Longdon took care to tread carefully in case traps had been set. He doubted it, however, as he had a feeling that he was meant to see what was inside the imposing stone building he was now approaching.

The doors were made of iron and the right-hand one swung open at his touch. Longdon found himself facing a pair of heavy black curtains, which he parted tentatively. Beyond was a scene that could easily have been lifted from any of the films Longdon had been watching over the last couple of days.

Along each wall, set at regular intervals, were torches of flickering flame. At the far end lay Sergeant Jenny Newham, manacled to a slab of grey stone, the heavy pendulum the landlord had mentioned poised fifteen feet above her ready to begin its descent, the curved steel blade so highly polished that it reflected the orange light from the torches like a mirror. Longdon breathed a sigh of relief when he saw that she was unharmed, then drew back in horror when he saw the grotesque tableaux of burned and mutilated figures that had been arranged in standing positions around her prostrate form.

"Welcome, Detective Inspector!"

The voice came from the shadows in the far left-hand corner. A voice not entirely unlike Richard Patterson's, but the tone was far more confident, flamboyant, theatrical.

"Patterson?" Longdon squinted but it was impossible to see who was speaking.

"I must confess," the voice continued, "I was starting to get a little concerned that you might not get here in time. Imagine that! Spend ten years constructing the greatest story Vincent Price never starred in and then have the climax ruined by the incompetence of the police force. Although I suppose I should thank you, really."

Now a figure stepped from the darkness, a figure Longdon recognised all too well.

"I see you're not that surprised to see me, Detective Inspector."

"No, Dr Valentine," said Longdon. "I am not, although I admit I'm surprised you're not wearing a cape and some theatrical makeup."

Valentine tutted. "Too over the top, my dear Inspector. I do have to make good my escape shortly and I should hate to trip over an unwieldy cloak. We real-life villains do sadly have to make some concessions to reality, hence the simple black suit you see me in. Much better for remaining unobtrusive. Oh, and it's Mr Valentine, by the way. I believe I already mentioned how particular we surgeons are about such things."

"None of that matters," said Longdon. "You're not going to get five miles without every available police unit on your tail. You may as well give up now."

"May I, Inspector?" Valentine smirked. "How very... television of you. Surely you realise by now that individuals such as myself always have an escape plan?" As he spoke he fingered the heavy lever next to his right-hand. "Now, I suggest you stay right where you are or I may be forced to begin my recreation of Roger Corman's The Pit and the Pendulum prematurely."

Longdon considered rushing him but Valentine was too far away.

"Just keep still, Inspector," said Valentine, "and no-one will get hurt. Well, no-one else."

"Are you all right, Jenny?" Longdon called.

"Fine, sir," came the muffled reply. "Just a bit... you know."

"She's unharmed and hopefully she's going to stay that way," said Valentine, taking a step forward to the first of the hideous figures. "You know, one of the advantages of being the pathologist on the case where you yourself are perpetrating the murders is that it is so much easier to get hold of the bodies afterwards." He tapped the blackened corpse on the cheek, causing it to wobble precariously. "Did you like my Alfredo? Poor old Andrew Wells, thinking he was off to a fancy dress party in his honour and instead finding himself swinging over the Avon Gorge."

"He wasn't your first, though," said Longdon, "was he?"

"Quite right, Inspector," Valentine replied. "That was, as you so cleverly worked out, Caroline Conrad. In fact, it was she who gave me the idea. When I was trying to decide how best to punish those who failed my Victoria I learned of her spinal implant. How delicious it would be, I thought, if she were shocked to death through it, just like in The Tingler. That film, I am sure you are aware, was made in black and white." He looked again at the charred remains of Andrew Wells, and then at the rest of the macabre tableaux. "But from there I decided that if the rest were to die, they should die in colour."

He moved to the second mutilated figure, the one with a gaping wound in its abdomen. "And so Dr Pritchard was despatched by the unicorn from The Abominable Dr Phibes. My God, his wife was boring, but it was necessary to strike up an illicit relationship with her in order for his demise to be achieved. Similarly, with Dr Davies, I had to spend interminable months under that clown makeup entertaining tedious children twice a week in order to recreate the scorpion death from Dr Phibes Rises Again."

He moved from the puffy, embalmed figure of Martin Davies to an empty chair. "But probably my proudest achievement was Lorraine Parsons. Can you imagine it? An entire scene from Witchfinder General recreated just for her! And she never realised it, or had the opportunity to appreciate it. And the burning by acid instead of flame was a masterstroke, don't you think?"

Longdon stayed quiet, not wanting to do or say anything that might endanger Jenny Newham's life.

"After that, Jasper Morgan was a bit of an anti-climax." He indicated the slumped corpse of an elderly man no longer in possession of his eyes. "But I had to have a scene from Theatre of Blood in my repertoire and it seemed the most appropriate. And finally..." Valentine's guide to the dead came to an end with the two people Longdon recognised as being the men he was supposed to be guarding this evening. "I realise I'm pushing things a little bit here, but in the original 1958 version of The Fly a scientist has his head and right arm exchanged with that of the title insect. Naturally I couldn't do that, but swapping these two gentlemen's appendages in a similar manner seemed a most appropriate way to deal with both of them at the same time."

Valentine surveyed his tableaux with pride, then he moved back to the heavy lever that operated the pendulum mechanism. "And now," he said, "for our finale."

"Before you go any further," said Longdon. "Could I just ask one thing?"

Valentine pondered for a moment, his fingertips resting on the lever. "Go on."

"Why?"

"I beg your pardon?"

Longdon gestured to everything around him while edging forward as surreptitiously as he could. "Why all this? Why such an elaborate way of dealing with the people you blamed for the death of your little girl? Why not just shoot the lot of them and be done with it?"

Valentine shook his head. "If only you could hear yourself, Inspector. Shoot them? The people who took my reason for living away from me? Who failed miserably to keep her alive for even a few moments once she was on the operating table? My dear Inspector, it is not for them that I have spent the last ten years planning and scheming, but for her, for my Victoria." There was the hint of a tear in his eye now. "When the whole story is known the world will never forget it. They will never forget the mad surgeon and the horrible way he murdered nine of his colleagues, but most of all they will never forget why I did it. They will never forget her. And that, Inspector, is why I have done all this. So that she will live on, in the minds of everyone who hears this horrific story. Then perhaps I can finally bury her."

"Her memory, you mean?" said Longdon, still moving closer.

"No, Inspector," said Valentine, wheeling out the figure he had hidden behind the bodies of Andrew Wells and Evan Pritchard, "I mean my Victoria. She is going to watch as her story - our story - comes to an end."

Valentine reached out, and pulled the lever. There was a grating of gears and the sound of heavy machinery being put into operation high in the building. Slowly, the heavy pendulum blade swung to the right, rising higher and higher until it was almost parallel with the ground. Then it stopped, hanging suspended in space.

"I do expect you to escape, you know," he said, addressing Jenny as well. "Otherwise it would hardly be a fitting end to the story, a story that would have no-one to tell it if at least one of you did not survive. However, I'm sure you will appreciate that I need to escape too -" he looked above him into the rafters "- and I thought this marvellous contraption the most appropriate way of killing... a little time?"

With that he pushed the lever forward and the pendulum began to swing, the distance between the blade and the helpless girl diminishing every time it passed above her body. Longdon rushed forward and began to grapple with the manacles that held her in place.

"My colleagues have the keys, Inspector," said Valentine. "But you're going to have to be quick."

Longdon turned to see Valentine taking one of the torches from its sconce and applying the flame to the already burnt form of what was left of Andrew Wells. Then he moved from victim to victim, setting them alight. They caught fire so rapidly it was clear they had been coated in something flammable.

"All that embalming fluid," explained Valentine as he moved to the corpses of Skilbeck and Marsden. "It works beautifully, as you can see. I think you'd better hurry."

Figuring that Valentine wouldn't have hidden the keys on the first corpse, Longdon instead ran to the ones at the other end that were only just beginning to catch light. He searched the pockets of Geoffrey Marsden and shook the corpse for good measure before moving onto Skilbeck.

"Getting warmer, Inspector," said Valentine with a chuckle as he made his way to the door. He pointed to the mummified corpse of his daughter, just beginning to char from its proximity to Wells' body. "I shall leave what is left of Victoria to watch over you. She always did enjoy a good ending."

And with that he was gone. Longdon was searching Martin Davies' corpse now, all the while batting at the flames which were beginning to spread across the floor. Nothing.

"Sir!" came Jenny's voice from behind the flames. "It's almost-"

"I know! I know!" Longdon risked a brief glance behind him to see that the blade was almost touching her. The corpses of Evan Pritchard and Andrew Wells were now so ablaze that all Longdon could do was kick at them helplessly. He'd lied! Valentine had lied! There were no keys here, none at all. He'd searched every victim, every one except...

Longdon turned to look at the empty chair intended to represent the absent body of Lorraine Parsons. Oh, very clever, he thought, giving it a kick. The chair fell over to reveal a set of tiny silver keys taped to the underside.

"Sir, I--"

"Coming, Newham, I'm coming!"

As fast as he could Longdon tore off the tape and ran to his helpless partner. The blade swung across once more and as he undid her ankles he could see that the next stroke would make contact. Her wrists were trickier and as he struggled with the final manacle the blade swept across her. She screamed as it slashed open her shirt, leaving a nasty gash on her belly. Then she was free and off the slab before the pendulum could continue its inexorable descent.

"You okay?" Longdon asked as supported her.

"Fine," said Jenny, her hand over her wound. "At least, I think so."

Longdon looked around them but there was no sign of Valentine. The walls of the building behind them were now a livid, flaming scarlet. They were about to get back to the car to radio for help when the roof fell in with a crash. Longdon paused. As well as the sound of destruction he could hear something else, above and beyond the noise of the collapsing building.

"Can you hear that?" he said to his colleague.

Jenny shook her head.

"Listen," he said. "I could swear someone's playing music."

Jenny concentrated and then, eventually, she nodded.

"Isn't that 'Somewhere Over the Rainbow', sir?" she said.

Longdon nodded and gave an exasperated sigh. Something told him the manhunt that would ensue after this would lead nowhere. Despite the very best efforts of everyone involved, this was one case that was going to remain open.

They weren't going to catch Dr... no... Mr Edward Valentine.

But the man in the raven-shaped hot air balloon that was currently soaring towards the horizon could have told them that.

The End

Acknowledgements

Firstly I must express my gratitude to Mr. Simon Marshall-Jones for saying yes to a project that has been on my mind for years. Thanks, Simon, for getting me to finally sit down and write the thing - it was every bit as much fun as I thought it might be and if I could I'd do it all over again.

Secondly, this book would not exist without the artistic endeavours of a group of individuals who helped to stimulate my imagination, thrill me, entertain me, and most important of all keep me sane when I was growing up. I've already dedicated this book to Vincent Price, but my inestimable thanks and appreciation are also due to the other creative personnel responsible for the films THEATRE OF BLOOD and THE ABOMINABLE DR PHIBES, namely Robert Fuest, Douglas Hickox, Anthony Greville-Bell, John Kohn & Stanley Mann, Louis M. Heyward, Michael J. Lewis (of Aberystwyth!) and James Whiton & William Goldstein. Thanks chaps - you really did all change my life for the better, and I cannot begin to tell you how much the movies you created mean to me.

Finally my thanks, as always, go to Kathleen, Lady Probert, who not only had to put up with me reading the entire text of this book aloud to her and acting out many of the scenes, but also had to endure my various Vincent Price impersonations as each of the characters from the films referenced in the text. Thanks, Kate. I don't know what I've done to deserve you, but it must have been something very good indeed.

About the Author

John Llewellyn Probert is the author of five short story collections, including the award-winning The Faculty of Terror and its follow-up The Catacombs of Fear (both from Gray Friar Press), Coffin Nails (Ash-Tree Press), Against the Darkness (Screaming Dreams) and Wicked Delights (Atomic Fez). Atomic Fez are also publishing his first novel, The House That Death Built, which continues the adventures of his supernatural detective characters Mr Henderson & Miss Jephcott, who first appeared in Against the Darkness. He lives with fellow horror author Thana Niveau in the east wing of a Victorian gothic mansion that they feel should be haunted. Sadly, so far they have yet to see a ghost, but that might be because what goes inside the house is already scary enough.

Lightning Source UK Ltd.
Milton Keynes UK
UKHW02f1908060918
328454UK00014B/802/P

9 780957 392700